The Split Circle

Robbie Dorman

The Split Circle by Robbie Dorman

www.robbiedorman.com

ISBN-13: 978-1-7336388-3-8

Cover design by Bukovero

For Maggie.

1

The van waited outside the train station. Rust ate away at it, every piece of trim rotting, bit by bit. A huge man sat inside eating a sandwich, his nose buried in a paperback book.

Tyler saw his breath in front of him. He dragged his luggage behind him, a carry-on he only just had time to pack. He pulled it through the snow towards the van. The driver didn't look up as he approached, and Tyler tapped on the glass. The driver's head jerked up, alarmed, and then he smiled, bits of fatty roast beef still stuck between his teeth. He rolled down the window. He was crammed into the cabin, a giant man, both in height and width. A massive mustache dominated his face, with crumbs caught in it. His eyebrows articulated, speaking a separate language as he spoke.

"American? Tyler?" he asked through a heavy accent,

one Tyler would know soon enough as representative of the English taught to everyone in Drastovia.

"Yeah, that's me," he said, forcing a smile. He shivered. He didn't have a jacket. He wanted to go somewhere warm and sleep off the hangover he could feel coming on. He had drank too much on the plane, to try to rest, hours and hours ago. He hadn't slept anyway.

"Door is open," he said. "Get inside, and I will take you to town."

Tyler pulled the van door open and climbed in, the interior no warmer than outside.

"Aren't you cold?" asked Tyler.

"You *are* American," said the driver. "Hello. I am Alex. Heat is broken. But it is short trip."

Of course it is.

"There is blanket in back, if you like," said Alex. "But is dog blanket. So probably shouldn't use."

"Thanks for the offer," said Tyler. So that's what the smell was, intermingled with the roast beef and onion sandwich that Alex still chewed on as he set down his book in the passenger seat and pulled away from the curb. The dirty train station stood empty. Only one other man had gotten off the train with Tyler. He had walked off, pulling a worn parka tight around him against the cold. Tyler never saw him again.

They passed sparse rocky hills, with clusters of trees breaking up dirt paths and dry stream beds. Small farmsteads, with ancient houses and Frankenstein systems of ramshackle buildings attached over the years rolled by outside. Assorted vehicles sat in the dust, some shiny and new, others decades old, thousands and thousands of miles driven into them. *Kilometers here, Tyler.*

"You play football?" asked Alex, staring back at him in the rear view mirror. *And soccer is football.*

"No," said Tyler, trying to deny his headache. "Not anymore. Referee now."

"Ah, I see," said Alex. "Makes sense."

"Why do you ask?" asked Tyler.

"Why else would you come here?" asked Alex, laughing, filling the van. Tyler saw Alex's breath as he laughed, great clouds of onion. His head started to hurt more. "You must have fucked up." More laughter, and Tyler wanted to scream at him that it wasn't his fault. He had done what he was told, stuck to his principles, and still, this was where he ended up.

He wanted to, but he didn't. He had done all that already, and it had changed nothing. He forced a slim smile.

"You could say that," said Tyler.

Marty had pulled him into his office after the meeting. Tyler had tried to stay calm, but he couldn't, barking at the long table of old men who banned him from the league. He had called them hypocrites, but it had not reduced his punishment.

"Quite a show out there, kid," said Marty, sitting behind his desk in his beaten up chair, the brown covering worn off.

"It's bullshit, Marty," said Tyler, pacing, his face still red.

"Sit down, kid," said Marty. "This isn't the end of the world, although it may feel like it."

"It's a death sentence," said Tyler. "You know it, I know it, they know it. I can't work anywhere. Rec leagues won't even let me work for *free*. I worked with him. That's it. They hired him, not me. I'm a fucking scapegoat."

"Tyler. Sit," he said, his voice weathered from yelling

across soccer fields for years. Tyler sat.

"How much does it mean to you?" asked Marty.

"It's everything," he answered, and he meant it. It had always been everything. His dad had bought him a soccer ball for his fourth birthday, when his mom didn't want him playing American football. Tyler was winnowy as a kid, tall, with long legs, and could run for days without getting winded. He led every team he played for up into college. And then both his knees exploded one day and he was never the same.

But he couldn't leave the sport behind. He rehabbed, and when he wasn't fast enough to play, he started reffing and worked his way up into the pro leagues.

"Because you're smart, you're young," said Marty. "It's not too late to pivot. You've shown a lot of resilience, but it's okay to move on."

Tyler stared at him.

"I can't."

"Alright," said Marty. "Then let me do some work, make some calls. I can find a spot for you, somewhere. Keep your head down, let yourself be forgotten, and you can come back, in a year or two."

"A year or two?" asked Tyler. "Jesus." He'd be thirty before he came home.

Marty had pulled some strings, asked for favors, and gave some in return, and got him a job here, in Drastovia, a neglected country between Romania and Moldova that loved its football, like anywhere else.

He hadn't slept in 48 hours. His eyelids began to creep down, even with the cold, the smell, and his headache.

The first plane had left Seattle on Wednesday morning,

and he landed in New York, and then London, and then again in Bucharest. Each airplane was smaller than the last. His final leg was a sixteen passenger tube that jostled in the air like a butterfly in a tornado. The lone child on board screamed the entire ride, and the passenger next to him threw up on takeoff. The man desperately crammed the barf bag over his mouth, stray specks of vomit splattering his hands and shirt. The smell still lingered in Tyler's nostrils.

He had four drinks crossing the Atlantic and took sleeping pills, but neither worked. The anxiety in his gut had nullified the narcotics.

The train from Bucharest had been calmer, but made his inability to sleep more frustrating. Every time his eyes closed, he saw the members of the board staring at him, condemning him. He would open them and stare out the window at the endless scattered trees and occasional small towns dotting the landscape. The hours droned on. He tried to read, but the words were meaningless. He opened up the language app to learn Romanian, but it was futile. The sounds passed right through him.

"That is statue of President Dragoi," said Alex, his voice booming, and Tyler awoke, seeing the sculpture he spoke of. Made of marble, it loomed over an empty park, a massive field of grass surrounding it. They approached the town, and it was denser here, with more buildings, more homes. The van shook as it hit a pothole, and then another. Alex muttered something in Romanian.

"Roads are bad," he said. "They spend money on statues. Not on roads. Roads would be better."

Tyler nodded. "Do you work for the football association?" asked Tyler.

Alex laughed again. "They do not care about us. Not yet. They will, though. No, I work for FC."

"What?" asked Tyler. He works for the local team, and he's picking up a referee? *Jesus, Marty.*

"Good job. I am thankful to Coach Vlad. He understand struggle of town. You will see."

Tyler saw well enough, as they passed into the city limits. Krav had seen better days. The van shook periodically as they hit potholes. They passed multiple carts pulled by solitary horses or donkeys, people staring at him. There were no sidewalks, and only the main road was paved. Various gravel roads led off in different directions.

"Where are we headed?" asked Tyler. They hadn't told him where he was staying.

"Mark will put you up," said Alex. "He lives on far end of town, in new apartment building. Very nice. You will see."

Tyler wondered what nice meant in Krav. Every building was on the verge of falling down. Retaining walls crumbled. They passed another beautiful park, this one ringed by a tall metal fence. Another statue stood inside, a soldier on top of a horse, with a sword pointing outward.

"Old war hero," said Alex, before Tyler could ask. "Gate is locked. No money for park attendant."

"What's that symbol?" asked Tyler. Circular shapes hung from every building, some small, some large, dangling from every house. Circles, with a line bisecting them vertically. "They're everywhere."

"The split circle," said Alex. "It's old symbol for town. Very important."

Tyler looked at them. His eyes connected with one, close, right outside the window. It filled his vision. Time slowed and all the distractions disappeared. His headache, the awful smells camped out in his nostrils, the anxiety of a new life in a new place, the exhaustion. All vanished. It captured him and kept him there.

Hundreds marched in the streets of Krav. They wore red hooded robes, and carried banners, banners bearing the symbol. They sang a song, a song of Krav, a song of sacrifice. A man walked in the middle of them, wearing centuries old clothing. An aura of terror permeated him, his eyes filled with tears. But he marched with the crowd, surrounded by them. They would feed the split circle.

And then they were gone. The van moved on, driving down the main road. Everything came back in an instant, and Tyler held back vomit, swallowing it. Tyler shook his head, the vision passing as quickly as it had arrived.

"You alright?" asked Alex. "There is plastic bag, if you throw up."

"No, I'm okay," said Tyler, taking a deep breath. The worst passed, and the van slowed down. Alex pulled into a parking lot of a small apartment building, off the main drag. It looked newer than everything else here. Tyler didn't know about very nice, but it didn't look like it was about to fall down, so nice would do.

"This is place," said Alex. "See? Very nice. Only best for our guests."

"Guest?" asked Tyler. "I'm just here to ref some football."

"I know!" said Alex, smiling big, his stained teeth showing. "What else is there in life? You are helping town. With you, we can play, and then we can win, and then we can *win*, you see."

"I call things down the middle," said Tyler.

"Oh, of course, of course," said Alex. "We all know! Krav is happy you are here! The split circle smiles. I will see you around! There is Mark. He will help you." And then Alex jumped out. Tyler climbed out, dragging his small luggage behind him. He could breathe again, the air fresh in town. And then the van door closed, and Alex drove away.

"So you met the welcome wagon, I see," said Mark. "Alex isn't the smartest guy, but he also smells terrible."

Tyler turned and saw Mark, slightly shorter than Tyler, with a face covered in a five o'clock shadow. He carried a little extra weight on him, but still looked in decent shape. He smiled.

"That was a joke," he said, extending his hand. "Mark Taylor." His accent was British, not Drastovian.

Tyler shook it. "Tyler Kenson. You English?"

"I am," said Mark, with a slim smile that could be confused for a grimace.

"How'd you get out here?," said Tyler.

"A story for another day," said Mark. "You're my assistant ref, huh?

"I guess so."

"I heard through the grapevine what happened to you. Lucky for you, Krav doesn't give two shits about your indiscretions."

"It wasn't--" said Tyler.

Mark waved him off. "Best if you don't tell me. Let's get you situated."

They went upstairs, and Mark showed him his room. It had enough space for a bed and dresser. They shared a bathroom.

It was small, but it was his. Tyler sat on his bed, feeling

it squeak beneath him. He opened the nightstand next to him. He pulled out the dog-eared mystery novel inside. Tyler flipped through it and a picture fell out.

"Oh, sorry about that, must have missed that when I was cleaning," said Mark. "Belonged to my old assistant ref. Sean. Irish guy. Nice enough."

Tyler picked up the picture. It was a man and woman, smiling at the camera, his arm over her shoulder.

"Why'd he leave?" ask Tyler. "Get promoted to the next league up?"

"Uh, no. You see, that's why you were called here, all of a sudden," said Mark, avoiding eye contact until he couldn't, finally meeting Tyler's eyes. "He disappeared. Vanished. Gone."

2

"This place is--" said Tyler, searching for the right word.

"A shithole," said Mark. "A proper shithole, if I do say so myself."

They were in their headquarters, a dingy three room office deep in an old building on the edge of town, a few minutes walk from their apartment. The white paint flaked off the concrete frame. It stood on a dirt field with scattered rocks and no grass. Stray dogs circled the small parking lot, a lone car parked inside.

The interior was worse. The carpeted hallway squished. Water dripped from multiple places in the ceiling. Tyler sunk into it with every step and he smelled mildew and mold. He grabbed the bridge of his nose, trying to ease his headache. He hadn't slept in 50 hours. He could make it until tonight and reset his internal clock. Mark had fed him a ham sandwich at their apartment, but the smell tested his gag reflex.

The bare concrete floors and walls of their office kept the mildew away, at least. A small antechamber split into two offices, one larger than the other. Desks dominated each room. Tyler remembered them from his middle school days, the ones used by teachers, supplied by cash-strapped districts. The drawer's lock would keep no one out, and the slightest touch would leave a ding or dent that would never come out.

"That one is yours," said Mark, pointing to the empty office.

"I guessed," said Tyler.

"You won't spend much time here," said Mark. "I only come in once a week, to check our schedules, email the league, and collect our paychecks, which are, before you ask, almost nothing. Still, the association gives us the office, so I use it. Don't look a gift horse in the mouth."

"That might be a little too complimentary," said Tyler.

"Hm, aye," said Mark. "It's an address, and somewhere to sleep when you get kicked out of your apartment because you called a foul on their star player and they burnt down your home."

Tyler's eyes widened, and Mark smiled.

"Oh, don't worry, hasn't happened here," said Mark. "In a past life, though. Multiple times. I've learned my lesson. The Krav FC pays for the flat, so I don't think they'll be burning it down. They might evict us, but that's a slightly less dangerous proposition."

"Krav FC is paying for our apartment?" asked Tyler. "I

had to leave the country because of accusations of fixing games, and now I'm supported by the local team. Lovely."

"They pay for our groceries as well," said Mark, smiling. "Don't worry about it, Tyler. No one's paying attention to us. Let's get the hell out of here."

"I'd love to go back and sleep," said Tyler.

"No rest for the wicked," said Mark. "You have more to see."

"Like what?" asked Tyler. His brain was foggy. His eyes ached.

"The pitch, you numpty," said Mark. "Let's go."

Tyler expected dead grass and small rocks, or the meme of a tree growing in the middle of the pitch. They pulled up to the most beautiful field Tyler had ever seen.

It was immaculate, bright emerald, vibrant, the color of the grass leaping at him, the brightest green he'd ever encountered. The bold, crisp white lines that dissected the pitch stood stark against the bold jade. It left him breathless. He'd seen many soccer fields in his life. He'd been on pro fields in the US. Tyler had visited London and visited the pro fields there, some of the best the world offered. They had stunned him.

Every one was different. Some were weathered from use, with the groundskeeping staff doing their best to battle against the army of cleats that cut through it, back and forth over the sod, the weather destroying what they fought to stay impossibly beautiful. Depending on the field, on the staff, they could lose. They *would* lose. Over the season, the turf would wear away. Stomping feet would destroy it.

Some would last longer. The grass would stay strong, withstanding the punishment of use. The green would stay bright and vibrant late in the season. But it wouldn't be perfect. It couldn't be. The abuse was too much, even for the best crews. Tens of thousands of steps take place over a single game, and over the course of a year, millions. Nothing could withstand that kind of trauma without showing wear or damage.

This field was perfect.

"How many games have Krav played this season?" asked Tyler. Mark stood next to him, their feet in the perfect, perfect grass.

"Twenty so far," said Mark.

"How many here?" asked Tyler.

"Half," said Mark.

He walked out into the middle of the field, every step an explosion of color and texture. He stood center circle. He felt the grass, the pitch, the game. Everything else fell away. Tyler felt like a child again, his virgin knees still able to sprint, to pivot, to turn on a dime. To dance the ball to the goal without complaint or reserve. He was a young dryad again, connected to the earth and field, this field. He would be a professional, he would be the next Messi, surpass the expectations of a US player, become the best--

"Makes you forget everything, doesn't it?" asked Mark, and Tyler was back, standing in the middle of the field again. His reconstructed knee ached from being jammed in a tight airplane seat for eighteen hours. He couldn't pivot and he couldn't dance. It worked, and it hurt, and it would never get better.

"This is impossible," said Tyler. "This town can't support this."

"You haven't seen it on game days," said Mark. "They

shake the earth. They found the money, even if they had to bleed for it, even if they had to starve their own children for it."

"It's amazing," said Tyler. The stands rose around them on all four sides, with luxury boxes featured prominently halfway up. "It's the best field I've ever seen."

"Aye, it is. I would hope it is," said Mark. "The town rots while the team prospers."

"And they don't care?" asked Tyler. He thought to the suspicious eyes as they drove him through town. To the carts pulled by horses and donkeys, the buildings on the edge of collapse, the massive potholes, and the crumbling retaining walls.

"Yeah, they care," said Mark. "They care about football. The stadium got the mayor elected."

"Should I know him?" asked Tyler.

"You will," said Mark. "He'll make sure of it. He pulls double duty. He was the coach of Krav FC, and now he's the mayor as well."

"I would call that a conflict of interest," said Tyler.

Mark laughed. "Of course it fucking is," he said. "Wait until you see who signs your paycheck."

"What? We get paid by Krav? The team we're supposed to ref?" asked Tyler.

"Who else can pay us?" asked Mark.

"The association," said Tyler, his headache ripping through his head. "I came here to clean my name. I can't get paid by the team I'm reffing!"

"Calm down, calm down," said Mark. "It's not a lot of money, to be fair. It's nice to get anything at all. This is Level 4 football, in Drastovia, for godssakes. No one's watching, no one cares. Every one down here is trying to leave. And if that means once and a while you look the other way on an offsides, then so be it."

"No, I refuse," said Tyler. "I won't be complicit in this. Goddamnit, Marty told me--"

"This isn't America, Tyler," said Mark, cutting him off. "There's three cops in Krav, and all of them are tucked inside the mayor's front pocket. A few thousand people live here, and all of them live and breathe football. Krav football. Coach Vlad promised a better team and he delivered. They were bottom of the barrel before he got here, and within two years, they're pushing for Level 3. They're going to get promoted this year if it continues, which is all anyone in this town wants. And I don't know who Marty is. I know the fellows down at the local association, who talked to other fellows, who talked to other fellows, who talked to your friend, and they all exchanged favors with each other, and you are here, and I assume it's because you love the game enough to pay your penance, because God knows you wouldn't be here for any other reason. But football is law here. If you behave, everything will go smoothly, time will pass quickly, and you'll get to go back with your slate wiped clean. But if you don't, it's not me you'll have to worry about."

"I'm not afraid of some hooligans," said Tyler. "I can handle myself."

"Hooligans are nothing," said Mark. "After the drink is through them, and the day is done, they go back to their flat, and they're nothing. If you call the wrong penalty against Krav, the farmer down the road will beat you in the street. This is their life, mate. So take your ethics and keep them safe under your hat, and pull them back out when you're home."

"I can't just turn off my ethics," said Tyler.

"The fella who you're replacing said the same thing to me," said Mark. "And now he's gone."

"Are you telling me he was killed?" asked Tyler.

"I'm saying that he did something wrong, and someone noticed, and now he's gone, and there was nothing he or I could do about it," said Mark. "Usually, by the time you're being told there's a problem, it's too late. I liked him. Didn't make a difference."

"So I'm just supposed to let them do what they want on the field?" asked Tyler. "I'll just let them punt the other players. Should be fine."

Mark smiled at that. "You haven't met Grigore yet. You'll be lucky if it's just a punt."

Tyler sighed. He walked away from Mark, out of the center circle. All his exhaustion, all his pain hit him like a ton of bricks. He couldn't do this. He'd go back. He could find work. He'd leave the sport behind. Move on.

Everything. That's what he'd said, what it meant to him. He looked down at the impossibly green grass, and the stark white lines cutting through it. No, he had meant what he said. He could navigate this. He would get back to where he was, before the conspiracy, before the scapegoat. Tyler could do it.

"Don't worry about it too much," said Mark. "Only a few games left to go anyway, and the season's mostly decided. Leave it to me, and I'll guide you through it." Tyler turned, facing Mark again.

"Why are you here, Mark?" he asked. "An Englishman, in Drastovia, in Krav? I know I fucked up. What did you do to end up here?"

"I have my reasons," said Mark. "But I'll keep them to myself. Best to keep you spic and span. Let's go up top. You've got to see the field from up high."

They climbed the stairs. Tyler's knee screamed by the time they arrived at the top, fifty feet off the ground. Mark's breath came a little short as they turned and looked over the field.

The color of the grass popped like a light bulb, illuminating the entire stadium in the fading light of the day. The argument with Mark seemed so distant now, seeing the field again, all at once. It still felt impossible. How did this small rotting place have this remarkable thing?

"Wonderful, innit?" asked Mark. "Almost makes all the shit worth it."

Tyler stared. The white-painted lines cut through the bright green, inscribing man's will on the earth. Here we play, and here we don't. There was nothing else, except those white lines. They were all we had to enforce order on nature, and we used it to play.

No, that wasn't true.

The game was life, was everything. Tyler realized, because he could see it now, from up above, what he couldn't identify from the ground. He had stood on that beautiful field, right in the middle of it. And now he saw the symbol of the village. It was on every building, hung from rafters and street signs.

The hooded masses now stood inside. The man with eyes full of terror now stood in the middle of the room. He stood on a dirt floor, in a room made of white stone. The crowd surrounded him, leaving him in a circle. The dirt was dark red, brick colored, and his hands trembled at his sides. He stared around at them, his eyes trying to find a familiar face among the crowd, but all of them remained hidden in shadow. His friends and family were there, somewhere, but he couldn't find them. They wouldn't help, because this was necessary to survive. For Krav to survive.

A figure came from the mass, joining the man. The man spoke, urgently, again, knowing his part but unable to stop himself from begging for his life. The glint of a dagger flashed in the figure's hand and he went behind the man, slicing vertically each limb, blood pouring down onto the earth. Pouring down into Krav.

Tyler blinked. Another vision washed over him, and he was back overlooking the field. *What was happening?*

He couldn't process it, his mind exhausted, but he knew something was wrong.

He looked at the field again.

It was here. It dominated the middle of the pitch. A circle, with a line bisecting it. The split circle.

Mark was already walking back down the stairs.

"Let's go see some local culture," he called over his shoulder.

Tyler only thought of what Mark had said earlier. "They live and breathe football." It was more than that. Their totems filled the town, their symbol of the game.

It was religion.

3

The sun was down, and Tyler wanted to sleep. Mark wanted to drink.

So they drank.

The bar was in the middle of town, not small, not large, a neon sign outside that read Bautura. Below it hung the split circle, this one made of metal, chain-link fence wire cut and sculpted into the totemic shape. The building was otherwise unadorned, and Tyler heard faint music from inside as they approached. He saw it briefly and then averted his eyes.

Tyler dragged his body behind Mark. It had been nearly sixty hours without sleep now. His headache had dulled, too tired to hurt, but his eyes closed on their own as they walked down the street. Mark insisted on them going out tonight.

"You need to see it the way it is now," said Mark. "Before

you ref a game. You'll understand."

"They serve food here?" asked Tyler, just outside. His stomach grumbled, his body craving calories if not sleep.

"Sure," said Mark. "It's edible."

As Mark opened the door in front of him, Tyler could hear the music, louder now, Foreigner coming from the bar's jukebox. Chatter hummed along with it, various conversations from the dozen or so people inside all creating a clatter, none of it in English. Tyler walked in behind Mark, his head tucked, hoping to remain unobtrusive, but he was tall, and blond, and distinctly a stranger. The buzz disappeared as he moved through the doorway. Everyone at the bar eyed him. His gaze danced around the room. The moment hung in the air, and he saw cold questioning eyes. He fixed his vision on Mark's neck, focusing on the blue vinyl of his jacket, keeping his vision there as Mark stepped toward a small table in the back. As they walked the buzz started building around him again, and he sat down across from Mark, and he looked up, and he could see the place now.

It was bigger on the inside and smelled like nicotine. Several men at the far end of the bar smoked, drifts roiling up to the ceiling from hand-rolled cigarettes. Decades old reports of Krav FC on yellowed newsprint concealed the wood-paneled walls. Framed kits hung on the walls from years past, some never worn, some with grass stains. Team history covered every piece of real estate. Then the bartender stepped into view.

Her black hair flowed around her like a veil. Her green eyes popped, alien artifacts on a human face. Her light brown skin was smooth, her movement behind the bar like a cat. Her gaze darted over to him, catching him, and he looked back to Mark.

"Who's the bartender?" asked Tyler.

Mark laughed. "First thing everyone asks," he said. "Maria. Owns and runs the bar. Given to her by her father, Vlad. The mayor." He raised his hand just above his head, a small wave to Maria. She noticed, walked over.

"Is there anything in this town not owned by the football club?" asked Tyler.

"You're precious," said Mark. "I already told you. Everything is football in Krav."

"Mark," she said. "I see you've brought in new blood."

"It wasn't all my doing," he said. "Maria, this is Tyler Kensen, the new assistant ref. Tyler, Maria Popescu."

She smiled, easy for her, only making her prettier. She extended a hand. Tyler forced himself to look into her eyes. He took it, her skin warm.

In that brief moment, Tyler felt something from her, something golden and warm. Her touch felt right. It felt like home.

"Going to keep the team on the straight and narrow?" asked Maria. Her English was perfect, her accent only slight.

"I'll do my best, I suppose," he said.

"American?" she asked.

"Yes," he said.

"And you came all the way out here?" she asked. "To little Krav? What trouble did you get up to, that you were exiled here?"

Tyler hesitated, not knowing what to say. He felt his face redden. Lack of sleep had made him sluggish. She stared at him for a moment longer and then laughed.

"I am only joking," she said. "We are happy you're here.

Football cannot continue without referees. And that is not permissible."

Tyler found his tongue. "Glad to be of service," he said.

Maria winked at him, and he could feel his face redden again. "Good to know. What can I get for you gentlemen?"

"Two Timis," said Mark. "And what's on the menu today? My boy Tyler is starving."

"Is he now?" asked Maria. "That's a good question." She dramatically posed, her hand on her chin. "For the American in town, only a cheeseburger will do. I'll be back."

Tyler watched her as she walked away.

"Be careful with her," said Mark.

"I--"

"She'll eat you alive, boy," said Mark. "She's the second most powerful person here, even if she likes to play the rebel."

"Who's number three?" asked Tyler, and then the door opened, and a massive man came in, followed by four others, all smaller. His hair was short, slicked back on top, shaved on the sides. His almost-black eyes scanned the bar. His shoulders strained at the tight fabric of his plain white t-shirt. He had several inches on Tyler.

"Speak of the devil, and he will appear," said Mark, his voice a little bit lower than before. "Grigore Ursu, star striker of Krav FC, and the third most powerful person in the town of Krav. He thinks he's number two, but don't tell him he's not."

Tyler watched as he grabbed a two-thirds full glass of beer off the bar from in front of one of the locals plastered there. The patron turned with an angry grimace until he saw it was Grigore, and then it vanished, and a sheepish grin replaced it.

He yelled in Romanian across the room. His voice boomed, filling the space. The assembled patrons all cheered. He yelled again, and Tyler still couldn't understand, until his last word, used as exclamation and punctuation.

"Krav!" he yelled, and he went to an empty booth with his group. Maria was right behind, a tray filled with beers and shots. Grigore grabbed her wrist as she left the drinks, and she slapped him across the cheek, a gunshot, the buzz disappearing again. Tyler tensed, ready to get up. Mark stepped on Tyler's foot hard, drawing his attention. Mark shook his head.

Grigore laughed and said something more in Romanian. The room filled with its drunken buzz again, and he let go of Maria's wrist. She left without a second glance.

"Is that normal?" asked Tyler.

"For him? Sure. Grigore would certainly be in some hellish gulag if it wasn't for football," said Mark. "For Level 4, he's great, and part of the reason the team has done so well this season and last. Vlad screwed his head on right, kept him *mostly* out of trouble. Mostly."

Then Maria was there, with two beers and Tyler's burger.

"Sorry about the wait," she said. "The Bear needs his attention."

"No worries," said Tyler. "Looks great."

"Made it myself," she said. "Anything else I can get for you?"

"I don't think so--" started Mark, and then Grigore was there, looming over them with a hand on Mark's shoulder. The muscles on his thick forearm rippled. He was the biggest football player Tyler had ever seen.

"Hello chicken," said Grigore, to Mark.

"Hello, Grigore," said Mark. "Prepping for the game tomorrow?"

"I do not need prep," said Grigore, smiling, all his teeth showing.

"It was a joke, mate," said Mark.

"Yes, chicken," said Grigore. "Who is this?" He pointed at Tyler. His finger hovered far too close to Tyler's face for his comfort.

"Grigore, this is Tyler Kensen. He's the new assistant ref," said Mark.

"Ohh ho ho, baby chicken, I see," said Grigore. "Hello, nice to meet you. I am Grigore. Best player for Krav FC. You--you are lowly referee."

"I--"

"Tut tut, baby chick does not chirp," he said, his finger even closer to Tyler's face. A sudden anger seized Tyler. He wanted to smash Grigore in the face. The travel and no sleep had destroyed all his patience.

"You will do right by Krav. Yes?" Still smiling like a hammerhead, Grigore nodded at him.

"I--"

"Or maybe you end up like last baby chick. Do you see him?" Grigore looked around, exaggerating as he looked left and then right. "He has vanished. Left us high and dry. We are lucky, you are here. And you will do right by Krav, yes?"

Tyler waited. "Yes," he said, when it was clear Grigore wouldn't interrupt him.

"That is good," said Grigore. "Then we will get along." He dropped his finger, finally, and with a small shove to Mark's shoulder, he was gone, back to his table, to more drinks.

"Smart," said Maria. She winked and returned to the bar.

"Chicken?" asked Tyler.

"Refs wear yellow here," said Mark.

"Deep guy, then," said Tyler.

"Oh, Grigore is a philosopher," said Mark. "And thank you for behaving. If you didn't, it'd be a lot of extra work for me."

"I'd hate to impose on you."

"I'd hate to carry your unconscious body home," said Mark, taking a long sip of beer. "He's a brute, but he's easy to please. Vlad is a little more complicated."

"What about Maria?" asked Tyler.

"What did I just say?" asked Mark.

"I have a pulse, what I can say?"

"I won't harp on you, I'm not your pa," said Mark. "But let me speak my piece, once and for all."

"Okay."

"Don't get involved with the locals."

"I--"

"Don't get involved. This is the only bar in town, and you can't help but come here. Maria is very pretty, and you're a handsome gent yourself. The locals--I know they've all given you the side-eye, but most of the people here are nice, kind, even if they forget about it if the team loses. You'll get to know some of them. Some of them *very* well. Maybe want to call them your friends. Don't. Krav is different, even from other cities here. I've been here for a while, and seen them come and go, and it'll be easier on you if you don't get involved."

A momentary silence fell between them, and Tyler searched Mark's eyes for meaning behind this warning. He saw nothing.

"Trying to protect you," said Mark. "It won't happen again. Eat your burger. I'm going to get drunk."

The food was good, and Tyler had a couple more beers, with Mark covering his tab. Mark drank twice what he did, while demonstrating no sign of inebriation.

"How can you drink so much?" asked Tyler, feeling warm. His headache had vanished, replaced with exhaustion.

"I'll tell you my secret, but don't tell anyone else," said Mark. He beckoned to Tyler, and Tyler leaned in. Mark leaned in as well.

"I'm very experienced at drinking," said Mark, loudly, and Tyler laughed despite himself. Another patron stumbled across the bar, a beer in hand. He slipped, falling down, the beer splashing onto Grigore and soaking his t-shirt.

He was up in a flash, showing a quickness Tyler didn't expect. He hauled the man off the ground, lifting him up into the air, a look of pure rage on Grigore's face. The drunk man was already bleeding from his fall, blood running down from a busted nose. Grigore pulled back a massive hand.

"Ursu!" yelled Maria, followed by a string of Romanian. Whatever she said, Grigore paused, the entire bar staring at him. He unclenched his fist and lowered the man to his feet. He then smiled, and pulled off his shirt, revealing a torso covered in hair. He draped the shirt over the man's shoulder. Grigore yelled again and the bar cheered.

"He ordered a round, for the bar," said Mark. "I think it's time we retired for the evening."

"Those are the best words I've heard in quite a while," said Tyler.

"Even I have a hard time keeping up with these heathens," said Mark. "And we have a game tomorrow."

"Looks like Grigore has the same thought," said Tyler, as Grigore and his crew went outside, the rest of the bar still celebrating their free drink.

"Give 'em a minute," said Mark. "Let them have some space on the street."

They gave them some time, and then they left, both of them walking through the cold night. They moved down the main road.

BAP BAP BAP. Heavy slapping noises became audible, getting louder and louder.

"What's that noise?" asked Tyler.

"I have a suspicion. Just keep walking," said Mark.

They continued, the noise getting louder. Tyler saw the source soon enough. Grigore and his men hadn't left the bar alone. They had taken the man who spilled the drink with them, and two of his crew held him while Grigore pounded him with his massive fists like a side of beef, still shirtless, steam pouring off his body.

"We have to help him," said Tyler.

Mark stopped Tyler, holding his arm with strength Tyler didn't think he had.

"No," said Mark. "We can't."

"They'll kill him," said Tyler.

"They'll kill *you*," said Mark, into his ear. "And we need to go before they see us."

"They don't have to see us," said Tyler, pulling Mark into a dark shadow behind a dumpster in an opposing alley. He picked up a nearby bottle and chucked it at a building across the street, near Grigore. It shattered, the noise echoing down the street, gaining the attention of Grigore and his crew. They stopped the beating. Grigore walked out into the street, looking for the source of the noise. Mark and Tyler hid behind the dumpster.

Grigore saw nothing, and then barked at his crew, who dropped the man to the ground. They walked down the street, Grigore beginning to sing loudly as they left. His voice trailed away as Mark and Tyler waited. When it was clear they were gone, they came out, going to the man, still groaning on the ground. His face was bloody, a mess of black and blue. His eyes had begun to swell.

"There's a small clinic, down the way," said Mark, and they picked him up, half carrying him down the street.

He groaned, but stayed conscious, and they left him with a nurse who spoke to Mark in Romanian. Tyler heard Grigore's name in the conversation, but stayed out of it. The nurse let them go.

They arrived at their apartment. Tyler was ready to sleep for a thousand years, and forget about Grigore and that poor man in the alley.

"No police report," said Tyler.

"No," said Mark. "Try and tell Vlad his star player was arrested the night before a game. The police would do nothing. That was dangerous."

"I couldn't leave him," said Tyler.

"Okay, boy scout," said Mark. "Get some rest. Big day tomorrow."

"Today wasn't?"

"Today was nothing. Tomorrow is game day."

4

The grass burned green.

"You ready for this?" asked Mark.

Tyler had slept through the night, twelve hours, and after eating a nice breakfast of eggs and bacon felt vaguely human again. The marathon of travel and discovery felt like a dream. They sat in their living room, small bags packed with their gear. Mark finished a bottle of water.

"I've reffed pro games before," said Tyler. "I think I can handle a Level 4 game here."

"You say that now. I've seen football in a dozen countries, and none of them feel like games here," said Mark. "Be ready for anything."

"I've seen riots, fires, fights--"

"I'm not talking about violence, hooligans," said Mark.

"Although, to be fair, there are plenty of them here as well. It's--" He sighed. "I can't put words to it. You'll understand after it happens."

"Anything else I should know?" asked Tyler.

"Yeah, don't call any penalties," said Mark.

"What?"

"Don't call anything. No offsides, no tripping, no pushing," said Mark. "I'll handle all the calls. Certainly tell me if you see something, but let me decide if we call anything."

"That's ridiculous," said Tyler. "Why am I even here?"

"It's your first game," said Mark. "Let me deal with it. Watch what I do. We can open you up a little bit, game by game. Don't be a hero."

"I don't need a lesson in reffing," said Tyler.

"You need a lesson in reffing *here*," said Mark. "Trust me. We need to get going." He pulled out two hoodies from a closet, gray and generic. "Wear this, and keep your hood up."

"Why?" asked Tyler.

"You don't want to be seen, coming or going," said Mark. "Just in case."

"Do I need a fake mustache too?" asked Tyler.

"Wouldn't hurt," said Mark. "You know where we can get some?"

They walked over to the pitch, a short walk. A few players warmed up on the field with hours to go before game time. Tyler followed Mark as they went into the locker room area. Scattered noises filled the hallways. Mark pointed.

"Home locker rooms down that way," he said. "Away over there. We're this way." He indicated straight ahead, and four doors down Mark stopped at an unmarked door.

Mark opened it, and inside lay their locker room, with three lockers along the wall, a bathroom with shower, and some chairs.

"The Taj Mahal awaits you, sir," said Mark, bowing as Tyler walked in.

"It looks fine," said Tyler. He turned as he heard Mark slide a deadbolt shut.

"Can't be too careful," said Mark. "Keep it locked. Five knocks to come in."

They changed into their uniform. Tyler donned the yellow shirt for the first time, along with long pants. Tyler had butterflies in his stomach. He always did. He had them when he played too, a nervous knot that would disappear when the game started. Mark disappeared out the door, leaving him alone. He locked the deadbolt, and he sat. He closed his eyes, and he breathed, a form of meditation, one he learned back in college.

He inhaled, and focused on nothing. Everything faded away. The travel, gone. The town, the split circle, the field, the bar, Maria, Grigore, Mark. All of it, gone. He exhaled.

The split circle surfaced in his mind. He acknowledged it, let it fade, exhaled again.

BAP BAP BAP. Grigore's massive fists beat the man's torso, steam rising off of him in the cold night. Blood erupted from the man's mouth. Grigore's teeth showed again, a mixture of rage and visceral glee. His eyes were wide, his pupils dilated as he punished the man, beat him for his mistake, a mistake, his fault, the man's fault, how DARE he--

Tyler breathed. He focused on the emptiness of his own mind and on his breath. In and out, in and out. The fabric of the chair, the stale smell of the locker room, the building beginning to vibrate. He let all sensation fade away.

He talked to Murphy only once, after Tyler found out about the allegations. He had to stop himself from throttling him, right there. The committee would convene the next day and hand Tyler his ticket to Elba. They had both been suspended, pending the meeting.

It was on Murph's front porch. Murph wouldn't let him inside the house.

"Hey Ty," he said, refusing to meet his eyes.

"Don't 'hey' me," said Tyler. "What did you do?"

"I didn't do anything," said Murph.

"Don't lie to me," said Tyler. "My whole career is on the line here, and you're lying to me on your front porch. What did you do? They're telling me I fixed matches, Murph, which I sure as hell did not do."

Murph sat down on one of the two wooden chairs on his small front porch. It was cold.

"How deep are you?" asked Tyler.

"Too deep," said Murph, finally looking up, meeting Tyler's stare. His eyes were wet. "I had to, Tyler. You don't understand. They were going to take a finger. They--they threatened Alisa. It was too much. I did what they wanted."

"You fixed games," said Tyler.

"Yes," said Murph. "I lied during the committee investigation, but I don't think it matters. They still know."

"You selfish bastard," said Tyler. "Who else is involved?"

"No one," said Murph.

"No one else?" asked Tyler. "You did this alone?"

"Not alone," said Murph. "With you."

"I didn't do shit," said Tyler.

"Yes, you did," said Murph. "You went along with everything I said. You followed up my calls, you backed my play. I told them you weren't involved, but they don't believe me. All the evidence supports that you're in on it."

"This is bullshit," said Tyler. Rage filled him. But Tyler walked away, before he did something he regretted.

"It had to be you," said Murph, chuckling. "It had to be you. You're the only one who wouldn't see it."

He looked back then, on the front walk of Murph's house in suburban Seattle and he saw the symbol there, the split circle, hanging from Murph's eave, directly underneath the door, and Murph was there, beneath it, waiting for him to come back, none of this was right--

KNOCK KNOCK KNOCK KNOCK KNOCK. Tyler jumped. The building thrummed, with heavy rain beating on the roofs. He got up and undid the deadbolt. Mark stood there.

"Is it storming?" asked Tyler.

"No," said Mark, with a smirk. "That's the crowd. It's game time."

Mark hadn't lied. Tyler had experienced nothing like this. As they emerged out of the locker room area, and onto the field, the stands were full, covered in people already singing and dancing. They all wore the crimson of Krav FC. Multiple men carried bass drums in the stands, beating them in rhythm. The clear day illuminated the perfect pitch. The green popped with every beat of the percussion, exploding in his vision. Tyler blinked it away.

Both teams warmed up on the field. Grigore stood in the center circle, the split circle, looking at the opposing team. His crew from the night before stretched around him. He peered over at Tyler, and smiled wide, devoid of humor or charm. Tyler broke first, and looked away.

Tyler stretched with Mark, doing short wind sprints. His blood pounded in his heart.

"There he is," said Mark, gesturing with his head. "That's Vlad."

Vlad looked unspectacular in his middle age, plain faced, slightly overweight with thinning gray hair. He walked with a subtle limp, his left leg always trailing behind him. He studied the other team, his eyes darting from man to man, assessing, looking for weakness. But he could have been anyone.

"Used to play, himself," said Mark. "He's from Krav. Once dragged the team to the most prominence it ever had, but was poached. Went to London. Played there until he hurt his knee and was never the same."

"Krav is gigantic," said Tyler. He had never seen a team that was so universally tall and broad.

"Vlad knows how it works down here," said Mark. "Grind it out with big fellas. Half of them imported. All that football money didn't go toward the field."

Grigore stood above them all. As the countdown on the scoreboard got closer and closer to game time, Grigore began to jump. Up and down, getting impressive height on each leap, higher and higher, gesturing toward the assembled crowd. The fans mimicked him, jumping up and down, and the stands shook.

"Where did all these people come from?" asked Tyler.

"Every house, hut, and shack within traveling distance," said Mark. "I told you."

A few scattered fans in blue stood meekly, fans of FC Rau, the opposing team. They occupied the bottom of the standings.

Mark spoke to each head coach. He spent more time with Vlad, with some gestures towards Tyler.

The clamor only built as the timer got shorter and shorter. As it hit zero, the drums beat and the crowd roared in support. Mark and Tyler took position.

The game started, and Tyler watched as Krav destroyed Rau.

Rau barely touched the ball. Krav was big, yes, but they also dominated possession, taking control and never letting go except to score. The first time they scored the crowd hit a volume that Tyler didn't expect. As Krav piled on the goals, he expected it to die down. It didn't. It only elevated, each goal louder than the last. The air horns, drums, and frenzied singing got louder and louder. The Krav players fed off of it, Grigore himself gesturing toward the crowd at every opportunity, his fierceness feeding into them.

Not that Krav played perfectly. Tyler saw mistakes in their game, but Rau wasn't talented enough to capitalize on them.

Not to mention the penalties. Tyler counted a half dozen offsides, tripping, and pushing penalties. Mark looked to Tyler, their eyes meeting across the field and Mark waved him off, every time. Mark called a single offside against Krav in the very beginning of the game, and then a few against Rau, but he, and by extension they, let the teams play.

The crowd did not stay silent. They became a force of nature, the noise and vibration shaking the earth. Tyler tried to ignore them, but it was impossible. He looked up and they were there. Chants and drums filled the air. Massive banners flew through the sky, all showing the split circle, drawn crimson red on a white field. Mothers held children as they chanted and sang. Men raised and lowered their arms, eyes closed. The fans wept, tears wetting their faces.

Krav destroyed Rau as they watched. Krav played physically, using their size to keep Rau off the ball. Any time Rau challenged, legs got tangled, or an inadvertent elbow was thrown, and the Rau player inevitably would be on the ground, beaten. By intermission Krav was winning 7-0, and as the game neared its end, they were winning 15-0, with Rau only getting a few weak shots on goal. Tyler's body ached, still not recovered from the day of travel. Mark waved him off at every penalty, and he was finding it harder and harder not to call anything.

With the game winding down, a younger Rau player caught a Krav winger napping and stole the ball, bounding down the field, the defenders out of position. It would be the best shot Rau would have all day, but the young player never saw Grigore.

Grigore's size was evident, but his speed was not, and his long strides caught him up to the player just before he kicked, blindsiding him. He minimally attacked the ball, but he hip-checked the player in the process, sending him flying, landing awkwardly on his neck and shoulder on the beautiful grass, leaving the young man dazed.

It was a clear foul, one that Tyler would have ruled a penalty kick. He didn't have a chance. Mark sprinted in and waved everyone off, allowing Rau to take the young player off the field. He cradled his arm, his eyes hollow. The crowd roared louder than ever. The Krav fans screamed in joy, with the Rau fans booing, the first real uproar they'd made during the match.

"Are we going to ignore that?" asked Tyler, in close to Mark.

"What did I say?"

"I--"

"No call," said Mark. "I'm keen on walking off this pitch. Look at the crowd."

Tyler saw a Rau fan get sucker punched by a Krav fan, and then dragged away by another Rau fan before they could hurt him worse, blood streaming down his face. Grigore gestured wildly, his arms pumping up and down. He moved tirelessly.

The Krav crowd acted as one, a sea of crimson. They swayed in time to the beat of the drums, chanting a familiar song, one they returned to over and over again throughout the match. The words filled the town. Tyler yelled just to be heard.

"This isn't right," said Tyler.

"This is not a hill to die on," said Mark. "We'll find one for you, don't worry. Let's get this game over with."

The fans only roared louder and louder as the clock ticked up. The game ended with no stoppage time. Grigore ripped his shirt off in the center circle, the crowd eating it up. Vlad stood on the sideline with no smile, congratulating his men as they came off the field.

"We should go," said Mark, pulling Tyler off the pitch. The Krav fans still sang and danced. Would there be any sportsmanship after the game, Tyler wondered, but Mark marched him off, his knees aching from the work. Mark pulled him into the locker room and they changed.

"Quickly," said Mark, throwing his normal clothes back on, a hoodie over top. Tyler did the same, his heart racing.

What was going on? Krav won, handily.

They were out of the arena in under five minutes, the door locked behind them and on their way back to their apartment, along with some dejected Rau supporters. Rau was just leaving the field. The Krav players still celebrated.

"Why are we running away?" asked Tyler. "We called almost nothing. We let them get away with murder. They crushed them."

Mark was less tense now, with them a safe distance from the arena. He walked at a normal pace, with the anxious expression on his face gone.

"Better safe than sorry," he said. "Because you never know. They might think they didn't crush 'em enough."

5

Tyler watched the town celebrate from their apartment window, overlooking the main drag. The town was raucous, buzzing, elated from the victory. People walked Ofranda Road, drinks in hand, banners and scarves held up high, waved in the air.

"What was that?" asked Tyler.

"I told you it was something," said Mark.

"That was embarrassing," said Tyler, the sea of crimson flowing below him.

"It was just a football match," said Mark. "You did fine. No longer a Krav virgin. You've been whetted."

"Why were we even out there?" asked Tyler. "Krav did whatever they wanted, and we just watched."

"You're standing there, aren't ya?" asked Tyler. "Enjoying

that beer?"

"Well--yeah," said Tyler.

"Then it was fine."

"It doesn't feel fine, it feels dirty," said Tyler.

"What was the final score?" asked Mark.

"Fifteen nil," said Tyler "But--"

"Could we have done anything to affect the result?" asked Mark. "Anything at all? Anything to give Rau a chance in bleeding hell to win that game?"

"No, but that should been a yellow against Grigore when he took out that kid," said Tyler. "At least. Probably a red. And he should have had a penalty kick."

"Kid was in no shape to kick," said Mark.

"His sub, whatever," said Tyler.

"Then maybe they score then, and it's 15-1," said Mark. "Still a colossal defeat."

"But Grigore would have the yellow on his record--"

"No one pays attentions to yellows from game to game down here," said Mark. "And it wouldn't matter, because both of us would be in the hospital, like the fellow from last night. Either the team, or more likely, the fans. They'd charge down on the field, and Vlad would let them, and they'd beat us. Only *beat* us, and not kill us, because Krav still won."

"I don't like it," said Tyler.

"It doesn't matter what you like," said Mark. "I'm sure you don't like being out in the middle of fucking nowhere watching a bunch of brutes kick a ball around, but here you are. You know the score. You do your time, keep your mouth shut, and pick your battles. Vlad knows what wins down here. He wants to move the team up, and with it the town. You're American, what do you care?"

"It feels like I'm failing," said Tyler.

"Your only job here is to make it out alive," said Mark. "Listen to me, I know from experience."

Tyler wanted to push Mark on why he was here in Krav, apparently here for the long haul, but the look in Mark's eyes dissuaded him. The game had taken a toll on both of them, and he didn't have the energy.

"Speaking of jobs," said Mark. "I got you a side-gig in town."

"A side-gig?" asked Tyler. "I thought assistant ref was my job."

"It covers your room," said Mark. "But you're not eating my food forever, and I'm sure as hell not buying you dinner again. I assume you want to eat?"

"Yes," said Tyler.

"It's an easy paycheck," said Mark. "George, at the south end of town. A fix-it man, handyman type. Machine, mechanic, all that."

"George? Is he from here?" asked Tyler.

"Born and bred," said Mark. "Solid guy, if a little strange."

"Strange how?" asked Tyler.

"For one thing, he hates football. Probably the only person in town who wasn't at the game today. Super smart. He's a good guy, once you get to know him."

"That's usually what people say about assholes," said Tyler.

"I never said he wasn't an asshole," said Mark. "You'll get along."

They drank beer, watching television as the evening wore on, the revelry outside not fading, even as the sun went down. Then the chanting started.

Tyler wasn't sure he heard it at first, a rhythmic background noise, far away. It grew around him, rising from the ground, surrounding him, filling the apartment, filling the town.

"You hear that?" he asked Mark, but Mark slept in his recliner, the light from the television flashing across his face. He was dead to the world.

Tyler pushed himself up from the love seat, walking to the window, looking out. He saw the torches first, and then the people holding them. They all wore red hooded robes, their torches scattered among the crowd, held above their heads, lighting the legion. They walked in step, down the main road, coming from the opposite end of town. They chanted, the rhythm rising around them, getting louder and louder. As they got closer, the song became clear. The one from the game.

The same as the vision.

They carried the same banners, long flowing white fabric, cotton, stained in red with the symbol, the split circle, next to the torches, held high above the sea. His eyes darted from one to the next, never the same but always the same, the same symbol despite the artist. Each pulling him in, a magnetic force that Tyler resisted each time, willing his attention away, only to be pulled in again.

Tyler watched out his window, down on the crowd. No one looked up, a sea of shadowy faces walking below him down Ofranda Road. Their loud footsteps matched the beat of the song. Tyler could hear their voices, individual tones rising to become one, an omnitone, a singular note that circled him.

Mark was still passed out. The crowd walked past, the

long river flowing down the street, over the broken pavement. But where did it flow too?

But the answer was there, before he finished asking. Where else would it go, but to the field, to the split circle?

They were headed for the pitch, and Tyler wanted to follow them, to see what they did. Because he realized at a primordial level that to know this town, he would have to see it. He would have to experience it. Not a football game, or going to the local bar. Once he walked with that red river, he would know Krav.

Then they were gone. The chanting fell away.

He waited at the window, time passing, but they were gone, and they didn't return. The song had vanished, and Tyler returned to the love seat, to his beer and the television. Mark still slept, softly snoring.

Tyler tried to watch TV, to forget the symbol burnt into his brain. Some sitcom played across the screen, but he couldn't pay attention, the laugh track roaring but Tyler's mind only saw the split circle, the mass of red robes.

What did they do in the split circle?

He needed to see, but he couldn't get up. A sudden terror filled him, a harrowing pain deep in his heart. Tears welled up in his eyes and he hurriedly brushed them away, denying them.

So he sat, letting the television wash over him, nursing his beer. After a time, Mark woke up with a snort, muttering a goodnight and then stumbling into his bedroom, closing the door behind him.

He turned off the television, and went to bed. He laid there, hoping that sleep would overtake him. He could think clearly in the morning. The symbol would be just that again, and the image of the crowd of people in red robes would just be that.

Tyler laid in bed, his body and mind still weary from travel, from the game that very same day, but sleep wouldn't come. Hours passed, and there was no relief. He got up, frustrated, and dressed, throwing on a hoodie, the terror that seized him momentarily now gone, and he left their apartment, walking out into the chilly night, his breath fogging in front of him. He zipped up his hoodie and threw the hood over his head, hanging down over his eyes.

He started walking, not toward the pitch, but toward the other side of town, where the red river began. He could not face the split circle, but he could face its origin. He walked, the pavement echoing with ever step. There was no one else out, the crowded road now empty except for him. It was late, but it wasn't *that* late. Did the red river sweep everyone away?

He walked up the road, past Bautura, into unknown territory. The road began to slope up, small row houses and fences lining the street. He looked up ahead, scattered streetlights following the route going up to the right, tracing up a hill, leading up and out of town. In front of him the ground rose, the road veering off from it, in fear of the earth. His eyes followed the hill up, a rising field of gravel and dirt, tufts of grass struggling to break through the rocks. On top of it sat a house, two stories and large, bigger than any other building in Krav aside from the football stadium itself.

It was old, made from white stone, the same white stone it sat upon, each mortared into place centuries ago. Despite its age, it looked impregnable, invulnerable. A steep roof rested on top, covered in sharp wooden shingles.

A man, sacrificed, surrounded by white stone.

It leaned over him, glaring down at him, seeing him for the outsider he was, full of anger that he dare fix his gaze upon it. Windows covered the front of it, circular windows, sixteen total, Tyler counted. Each had a lit candle in it, burning against a dark background, sixteen eyes of flame staring out at him.

He was looking for it without realizing it. As he had walked up to the house, he had looked at each passing home, and he had found it. The split circle was on every one. He couldn't find it on the Stone House. His eyes searched, looking for it hanging from the roof, from the eaves. And then he saw.

Each circular window was bisected by a simple line, straight down the middle. The candles' light completed the image. The symbol was integral to the house's construction. They were not adornment, added later, hanging like a wind chime or a dream catcher. They were essential.

"It's not safe to be wandering alone, so late at night," said a familiar voice, from nearby. Tyler looked to its source, one of the houses bordering the road, under the shadow of the house on the hill. A porch, with a small bulb creating a halo of light. He walked towards it. It was Maria.

She held a smoldering cigarette between her fingers, a trail of smoke bleeding into the sky. She wore a simple white house dress. She looked stunning.

"I couldn't sleep," said Tyler.

"It was a busy day," she said. "Big victory."

"Were you at the game?" asked Tyler.

"I'm at every game. My father is the coach."

"I know," said Tyler.

Maria raised an eyebrow. "You should have given Grigore a yellow."

"I don't think he would have taken too kindly to that," said Tyler.

"Oh no. He would have bludgeoned you to death in front of everyone. And they would have cheered. But you still should have done it."

"Not sure if that's the best start to my career here in Krav," said Tyler.

Maria shrugged, flicking her ashes into a nearby ashtray. "It'd get you out."

"Do you not like it here?"

She paused, staring at him. "I prefer the city," she said.

"Then why are you here?" he asked.

"Good question," she said. "Mostly my father. This is home to him. And he asked me to stay with him. To help. So I did."

"But not home to you?" Tyler asked. He stood at the base of the steps leading up to her porch, looking up at her. The glow of the lone bulb surrounded her.

"Home is London," she said. "But there have been Popescus in Krav for centuries. So I understand why we came back."

"Would think you'd be at your bar," he said, one foot on the first step.

"No purpose," she said. "No one would be out this late on a night after the game."

"I saw the--procession, I guess," he said. "What is that? I've never seen anything like it. It was creepy. Reminded me of--"

"Church?" she asked.

"I was going to say a cult," said Tyler.

Maria shrugged again. "It is tradition here in Krav, dating back a long time. You honor the game, the earth. Honor the town."

"So you were in the procession?"

She laughed. "No," she said. "Football is a means to an end."

"To what?"

"To grow Krav. To truly build it into something, we need capital. And football is the quickest path to it. The people here think the chants, and the robes, and the whatever, that they help the team, help the town. Who am I to argue?"

"It seemed a little strange to me," he said. "And the symbol everywhere--"

"Krav is old," she said. "And old traditions seem strange to people who come from young places."

"That's fair," he said. "Do you know anything about that big house?"

"It's very old," she said.

"And that's it?" he asked.

"It's very old, and no one lives there. It's public property," she said. "You have a lot of questions." She took a drag from her cigarette.

"I mean, I've been in town less than a day, and Mark won't tell me anything except where to get drunk and how not to call penalties."

"Patience is a virtue," she said. "Krav will present herself to you, in time. You just have to pay attention." She smiled and put out her smoke. "Would you like to come inside for a drink?"

"Just a drink?" he asked.

"A drink to start," she said, smiling again.

"Grigore won't mind?"

"I don't belong to anyone but me," she said. "Not my father, not Grigore."

"He seemed awfully possessive of you last night," said Tyler.

"Grigore thinks he owns everything he touches," said Maria. "He is incorrect."

Don't get involved, Tyler. Mark's words sprang into his mind. The same anxious fear from before, from when he saw the river of red robes was there again, and he didn't know why. A beautiful woman was asking him inside, and every part of him was telling him to take her offer. The house on the hill still stared down at him.

"I would love to," he said. "But it's probably better if I practice that patience you were preaching."

"No fun," she said. "I don't bite."

"Just call me old fashioned," he said. "But I'll be around."

She extended a hand, and he took it. She didn't shake, only holding it for a moment. That same golden feeling returned. His head buzzed, like he was drunk.

"Don't be a stranger. And get some sleep," she said. And she went inside, the small bulb turning off a second later, leaving Tyler alone in the night with the house on the hill, its candles burning.

6

"Krav is a great and old city, and look what it has become. Football is a scourge upon the Earth. It should be forgotten, and left to die in the dust."

George talked as he worked. Tyler cleaned and organized the vast piles of junk George kept behind his shop on his first day of work. George worked on a fridge, the back exposed, a light strapped tight around his bald head. It gave him the appearance of a caver. Grease stained his hands black. He spoke freely, with no shortage of words, pouring them into the broken fridge, where they bounced out at Tyler. Tyler would learn that George didn't need help at his shop. George really just wanted someone to listen. More accurately, George wanted someone to pour words into.

"You, young man, you listen to this," said George. "My

family is an old Krav family. We have been here as long as Krav. Before Krav. Before anyone! And never has it been in worse a state. I cannot even drive my truck down the road without hitting a pothole! And does Vlad do anything? No! He coaches his team of brutes to win football matches, to terrorize the town, as our infrastructure crumbles!" As extra punctuation, he pulled a piece of metal from the back of the fridge and threw it to the concrete floor of the shop.

Tyler had arrived early as instructed, struggling to wake up after attempting to sleep the night before. Two cups of coffee helped a little.

The split circle confronted him with every step. They hung from every doorway and rooftop. Tyler had tried not to think about the harrowing visions. They hadn't reoccurred after his first day here, which was sleep deprived and anxious, but he tried to avoid them at every step. But his eyes had caught one as he walked in the early morning.

The woman laid in the circle, the same circle as the man had bled into. She wore more modern clothing, and only a few people surrounded her. She was beautiful, lithe, with long legs and arms, with long flowing raven-colored hair. She wasn't bound, but her eyes contained fear. She spoke in an alien language, not Romanian, something else, directly to Tyler, into his eyes. Tyler spoke back, in a language he didn't know, and she nodded. She looked up, her eyes fearful but determined.

And then she shook, her hands gripped into hard fists, her body convulsing on the brick colored dirt, the earth saturated with blood. She shook, and then her eyes opened, her nose bloody. The fear had vanished from her eyes. Something else was there now.

Tyler returned to his mind in the early morning with a

gasp. Krav was doing something to him, but he didn't know what. He kept his eyes on the ground for the rest of the journey. He did not mention his visions to George.

He was at the address given at 7 AM. He was there alone, though, the door locked and a pulldown metal gate over the top of that. It was dark inside. Tyler waited.

Twenty five minutes later George walked up, his shambling footsteps echoing down the empty street. He came into view, a slight hunch obscuring his height. His wrinkled forehead led the way, lined from years of squinting at small things. He wore dirty overalls over a stained white shirt, worn tennis shoes on his feet. No sweatshirt or sweater to cover against the morning chill. His arms were like Popeye, thick forearms and slender biceps.

He saw Tyler and then barked something at him in Romanian, a dour look on his face. It didn't sound friendly. Tyler put on his most earnest smile and extended a hand.

"Hi, I'm Tyler Kenson. Mark arranged for me to work for you," he said.

"Oh. American?" he asked, glancing up at Tyler before bending over to unlock the metal grate that covered the facade of his shop.

"Yes."

"Fuck America," he said, casually, the invective second nature to him.

"I--"

"Come inside," George said, sliding the grating with crooked fingers. George unlocked the front door and went in, with a small ring sounding as it opened. Tyler followed him.

George flipped on the light, and the fluorescent bulbs

blinked on with an audible hum. The storefront was simple, a walk up counter, with one side lined with larger appliances, fridges and washers and dryers, fixed and ready to sell. Shelves covered the other wall. Radios, blenders, and toasters sat on top of it.

"You'll work out back," said George. "You don't handle the money."

"Got it," said Tyler. They continued into the rear of the shop, passing through a set of swinging doors into a half-open workshop. Tyler stood in a small open area in the center, surrounded by islands of tools, toolboxes, and junk.

"Clean. Organize," he said. Tyler couldn't place his accent, unlike any others he'd heard so far. It was alien and homeless. "Keep like things together. Do your best. I do not expect miracles."

George left him then, and Tyler started working. He rolled up his sleeves, his hands immediately filthy. He should have brought gloves. George reappeared after a time, and began tinkering with the refrigerator, at least two decades old, the front doors slightly tilted.

Shortly after he poked his head into the back of the fridge, a question came.

"You are a referee like Mark?" he asked. It took a moment for Tyler to realize George was talking to him.

"Yes," said Tyler, collecting gears and piling them together.

And that was all it took. George was off to the races.

"You see it, don't you?" he asked.

"See what?" asked Tyler.

"The degradation of my town!" yelled George.

"It seems run down, in places," said Tyler.

"Run down, bah," said George. "It is collapsing before our very eyes. And yet we build a field. A field! We could invest in the roads, or in agriculture. In green technology, look to the future! But what does Vlad do? He invests in football. He invests in grass!"

"The town seems to like it," said Tyler. "Everyone is invested in it."

"Of course they are," said George. "It is something, more than we had under Stroescu. He gave us nothing but bad textbooks, bad money, and the English language. So they take it, and they become proud of it. But there are other ways. Vlad is smart, he should know that. Do you approve of it?"

"I don't think it's in my place to judge," he said. "I'm an outsider."

"But you love football? You must," said George. "Why else would you participate in it here?"

"I do," said Tyler. He answered it without pause. It was why he was here. He loved the game. Tyler would do anything for it.

"How? Why?" asked George. "It contributes nothing. It is empty."

"That's not true. It's pure. It's simple. You have a field, and a ball, and you have the game. It can't be explained, the art of it. When I watch it, when I play it, when I ref--I feel like I'm linked. Not to just the team I'm rooting for or playing for. Even when I referee. It feels like I'm connected to everything. Nothing else I've ever experienced has done that to me."

George had taken his head out of the back of the fridge, grease spots on his face, his hands covered in it. He peered at Tyler, and Tyler thought maybe he had gotten through to him.

"You're an idiot," said George, and he returned to the refrigerator, his fingers rummaging through the parts inside. He soon launched into another tirade against something Vlad had done, switching between languages as his anger overtook him. Tyler cleaned.

Lunch time came, and George put down his tools and walked to the large sink. He turned on the water until steam rose and lathered his arms up to the elbow with lava soap. The grease came off black in the water, circling the drain.

"Kid, lunch," he yelled. "Clean yourself."

George went to the front and returned with a paper bag clutched in the crooked fingers of one hand and a thermos in the other, plastic cups tucked between digits. He walked out into the small yard of scattered grass and rocks behind the workshop, where a wooden patio table was set, two chairs with it. George sat, and gestured toward the other. The warm sun dispelled the chill in the air, and the sky was above them.

He pulled out of the bag another plastic bag, filled with many small dumplings, piled on top of each other. He revealed another container, and then smoothed out the paper bag and emptied the dumplings out onto it. George revealed another container and popped the lid off. Sour cream.

"Help yourself," he said. "Use your hands. I am not squeamish."

Tyler grabbed one between thumb and forefinger, the dough of the dumpling soft and cold to his touch. It was simple, wrapped and twisted at both ends, a small pleat in the center pocket. He took an exploratory bite, half of the bundle of dough in his mouth. George poured them both a cup from the thermos. His eyes watched Tyler.

The flavor of the cold dumpling in his mouth was incredible. The mixture of meat, spices, and the simple, earnest flavor of the wrapper amazed Tyler.

"How is it?" asked George, handing over a cup of the steaming liquid to Tyler.

"It's wonderful," said Tyler. "Where'd you get these?"

George smiled at that, the first smile Tyler had seen from him. "Homemade. My own recipe. Have some tea. Hot tea on a cool day."

Tyler finished his dumpling and took a sip. Soon his stomach was full of dumplings and tea. It was the best he'd felt in Drastovia, with the warm sun shining down on them.

"Did you mean what you said?" asked George. "About football?"

"Yes," said Tyler. "Every word."

George nodded. "You are a believer. That is both very good and very bad."

"Why do you say that?" asked Tyler.

George sipped his tea, the steam rising over his hard, sunken eyes. "Do not trust Mark."

"What?"

"Do not trust him. He can be very charming, but you are only here to cover his ass. Why do you think he is here?" asked George.

"I don't know," said Tyler. "He wouldn't tell me any specifics."

"He is here because of Vlad. They are close. Or at least were." He gestured with his hands. "Now? I don't know. Things have happened. But they were good friends, in England, on the prodigal son's great journey to the West. Vlad had something on him, kept Mark in his pocket. And now Mark works for him here. And that will be you, if you are not careful."

"Why are you telling me this?" asked Tyler.

George looked up, at the clear sky, and around him, at the small plot of dirt they sat on. "When I was young, Krav was a better place. More people, more money, more jobs. It was not a backwater, a place where people snicker when they hear the name. They laugh at us now, they do. That is one thing that I agree with Vlad on. He wants to silence them. But he will do anything to make that happen. But it will not be easy, making Krav whole again, making it what it once was. But Vlad disagrees. He thinks football will be quick, a shortcut to past success. And I do not trust any man who seeks a shortcut. It is only right that you know where you stand."

"I'm just here to ref some football," said Tyler. "I don't want to get involved in anything more than that."

"But *everything* is involved," said George. "Vlad has made sure of that. Your own words. Connected to everything."

"You mean that symbol, the split circle?" asked Tyler. "The procession out to the field the other night?"

"That is a corruption of Krav," said George. "The symbol, as you put it, the ritual. Those are old. Old when I was a small baby. They have existed in Krav for a long time, before the town had a name, they were here. They kept our coffers full, and our houses warm. They insured the safety of our children. But we fell away from it, and Krav fell apart. But Vlad has connected them. Made them about a game." George shook his head. "It is so much more than that. They truly are everything. And this corruption is why I cannot stand by him. It is the old way. Football does not deserve its blessing."

"What about that big house on the hill?" asked Tyler.

"It is a remnant," said George. "Of old Krav. It was a meeting house. Now, it is used only by Vlad, and his inner circle. It is a shame. Everyone was once accepted there. Now it is a just a tool, wielded by Vlad to divide his followers."

"Followers?"

"That is what they are," said George. "He is a pied piper. And they follow happily."

"You don't have the symbol anywhere," said Tyler. "Everyone else does." Tyler thought of mentioning his visions, but thought better of it. George would think he's crazy.

"Not anymore," said George. "It doesn't mean what it once did. Everyone else can follow Vlad into whatever he has made. I will stay behind, like before."

"You knew Vlad?" asked Tyler.

"Yes," said George. "I am surprised he hasn't talked to you yet. He'll want to drop you in his pocket."

"I'll keep that in mind," said Tyler.

"You must think I am an old coot," said George.

"I don't know what to think," said Tyler. "I just want to do my time, and get back home."

"Krav is home to me, so I understand," said George. "I will help, if I can. But do not think I will take it easy on you. All I have in my life is Krav, repair shop, and dumplings."

"They are some damn good dumplings," said Tyler.

"It is good that you like them," he said. "I have many more. You need to eat. You are skin and bones. Let us work."

And with that, lunch was over. George spoke still as he

worked, the fridge his microphone. He talked more about football and everything that crossed his mind. Tyler let his thoughts wander as he cleaned and straightened up the shop. About what George had said, about Mark, about Vlad, about the split circle. The old man believed what he said. Tyler was sure of that, but not of anything else.

Tyler could only be true to himself. That's all he had to go by. Nothing different than at home.

The split circle still hung at every door as he walked back to the apartment. He averted his eyes. He couldn't explain the sense memories they provoked, but he could feel them burrowing inside.

The same steps he took taken by the town en masse, dressed in red robes. All normal here. A part of Krav.

7

Krav was deserted. Ofranda Road was empty. Tyler looked out in the early dusk light and saw nothing.

There was an away game.

Mark had already left for the night, saying he had personal business to attend to, leaving Tyler to his own devices. The team bus had departed early that morning. The rest of the town trailed it, with people crammed into vans, aged sedans, and anything with an engine that could make the trip.

Tyler went to Bautura, unsure if anything in town would even be open. As he approached, Tyler could hear a faint tinkling of guitar from within. He made sure not to look at the split circle.

He opened the door, and a lone man nursed a beer at the bar. Acoustic folk music came from the jukebox. Maria popped up from behind the counter.

"Well, hello," she said. "Gracing us with your presence tonight?"

"Surprised to see you," said Tyler. "Shouldn't you be at the game?"

"To do what? Cheer like a good girl?" she asked.

"I--" said Tyler.

"I do not need to attend my father like a servant," she said. "They will do fine without me. You should sit."

Tyler took his pick of the tables, and Maria came over to him. She had dressed simply, in beige pants and a blouse, her hair tied back.

"What do you want?" she asked.

"The same as last time," he said.

"We are out of beef," she said. "So I cannot make a cheeseburger."

"What else do you have?" he asked.

"Do you trust me?" she asked.

"Is that a trick question?"

She rolled her eyes. "Say yes, and you will get dinner."

"Then yes," he said.

"Okay," she said, and then she disappeared into the back. She returned with a tray. She set it down, handing him a beer and a steaming bowl of soup with some buttered toast on the side.

"Here, eat," she said. She sat across from him.

"What is it?" he asked.

"Do you trust me?" she asked. "Eat. It is not poison."

He took a sip of the broth, blowing softly at the rising steam. It was yellow, fragrant, with vegetables and thin strips of meat floating in it. It smelled great.

The taste was spicy, hearty, but good. He chewed some of the meat. It had a subtle savory flavor. A little rubbery, but not bad.

"Do you like it?" she asked.

"Yeah, it's good," he said. "Will you tell me what it is?"

"It's tripe soup. I cannot take credit for the recipe."

"And tripe is--"

"Stomach lining of a cow, yes," she said, smiling.

He shrugged and swallowed, eating another spoonful. He had eaten worse, and it tasted great. He took a long sip of the beer. It felt nice.

"Aren't you going to introduce me?" asked Tyler, gesturing with his head to the man sitting at the bar.

"That is Marius. He does not speak English, and he hates conversation," she said. Marius said something in Romanian and Maria replied. He laughed and focused again on his beer.

"Sounds wonderful," said Tyler.

"He's the perfect customer," she said.

"I guess I'll be quiet then," he said.

"You do have other appeal."

He didn't know how to reply to that. Tyler wasn't shy by any measurement, but Maria inspired it in him. He took a sip of soup instead.

"How is George treating you?" she asked.

"You know about that?"

"Of course," she said, with no further explanation.

"He's treating me with what I imagine is kindness, for him," said Tyler.

"Has he fed you his dumplings?" asked Maria.

"Yes," he said. "They're amazing."

"They are," she said. "He won't give up the recipe to me, no matter how many times I ask. But that means he likes you. Most don't even get a sniff of them."

"He doesn't talk too kindly about your father," said Tyler.

"He is not alone," said Maria. "And George has his reasons for disliking my father. I understand them."

Tyler's tongue hummed from the peppers in the soup. He had finished it.

"Well?" asked Tyler.

"Do you want all my secrets?" she asked. "Because some of them have a price."

"Only this one, for now," he said. "And how secret can it be? It seems everyone in this town knowns everything about everyone."

Maria raised her eyebrows. "That is not true. I know more than most. And I will tell you, but you cannot tell George I told you. He is vain about his hurt."

"Mum's the word," said Tyler, and zipped up his lips, throwing away the key.

"George and my father were friends, as children. There were more people here then, but still not many. They were similar ages. Both lived under the dying days of Stroescu's reign. My father was an excellent football player, but leaving was out of the question. All talent remained inside the country, unless they defected. It was dangerous, and my father was happy here. He was the best player in Krav, the best player Krav had ever seen. Better than Grigore. There is no footage of him as a player. But he would play for Krav, and play for Drastovia, and be rewarded for it. George was smart, but he was not an athlete. And then Stroescu fell."

Tyler was only vaguely aware of Daniel Stroescu, a dictator of Drastovia up until the mid-80's, when he was deposed, assassinated, and the country changed to a form of democracy that had held ever since.

"And your father left," said Tyler.

"Yes," said Maria. "With a new opportunity right in front of his eyes, he couldn't turn it down. He left Krav, with offers from multiple European teams. He bounced around a little, and then settled in London. That's where he met my mother. He played, was starting to make a name for himself, and then he got hurt. Blew out his knee. I was born by then. Surgery, rehab, blew out the other knee. More surgery, more rehab, but he was no longer the same man."

Tyler's hand reflexively went to his own knees, the heavy knot of scar tissue covering the back of each.

"I grew up. He found work. Mother passed. And he remembered Krav, and we came back. But George never left. He stayed, opened his repair shop, and watched his town fade. He did what he was supposed to do. But it did not matter to Krav, which lost money to corruption and indifference. My father returned, happily accepted as new coach. Then as new mayor. With a return to the old ways."

"I mean, it seems like it's working," said Tyler.

"Yes," said Maria, smiling.

"Your influence?" asked Tyler.

"Since you are talking to me, yes, clearly. But do not ask my father that question."

"And George resents that?" asked Tyler.

"Yes," said Maria. "And I do not blame him. I enjoy talking to him, even if I can clearly see he does not want to engage too much with me. But for Krav to be a place of worth again, the old ways must become new. And the fastest way for a town to become a city to become a power is through sport. They see strength on the field as strength in life. And they are not wrong."

"Even if that means looking the other direction as Grigore beats a man in the street?" asked Tyler.

"I make no apologies for the Bear," she said. "He is my father's problem. I am not an animal handler. But yes, even that. Sometimes sacrifices must be made for life to improve."

"Does that include you?" asked Tyler.

"Well, I am here," she said. "And I could be anywhere else."

Marius said something again, and Maria responded, standing up. She took Tyler's empty bowl and bottle. She poured Marius another beer, and returned with a second for Tyler.

"Thank you," he said.

"Remember this the next time you spurn my advances," she said.

"Hey--"

"It is a joke, Tyler," she said. "I understand your hesitation."

Tyler smiled, and wanted to say something, but bit his tongue. He took a long swallow of beer, letting the flood of alcohol carry his words away.

"I will not hide my interest, like a fettered nun," she said. "Another way to control. I will not allow it."

Tyler had words now. "I never said I wasn't interested. Only not at that time. I've had a lot on my mind, and it wouldn't have been fair to you."

"On your mind? Like your career as an assistant referee in Krav, a small town in Drastovia?" she asked.

He looked at her. The thought of his visions flashed through his mind before he answered. The visions of the split circle.

"I mean, yes," he said. "More about if it's worth it in general."

"It is a simple question," she said. "Return on investment."

"You say that--"

"Is it valuable to you? Why are you here?"

"Because I love the sport, and I can't fathom my life without it," he said.

"You sound like my father," she said.

"Jesus."

"My father is a good man, despite what anyone says," she said. "Even if I often do not like him."

"Does that stand for me, too?" asked Tyler.

"I don't know yet," she said. "But I already like you a great deal more than my father."

"Glad to hear it," he said. "Have you heard how Krav did today?"

"They won," she said. "4-2."

"Close game."

"Expectations for away games are different," she said.

"You mean they don't have refs in your dad's front pocket?"

She ignored him. "A win is a win. And everyone is much happier after a victory, rather than a loss."

"Do they still march through the town?" asked Tyler, half-joking.

Maria didn't see the humor. "Yes. They do," she said, her eyes avoiding his. He had said something wrong.

"Is there anything else to do around here except watch, play, or referee football?"

She looked back at him. "Besides drink?"

"Yes," he said.

"Like on a date?" she asked, teasing him.

"For example," he said.

"Not really," she said, laughing. "There is football and football and football. I like to go for drives in the country. There are some pretty views."

"That's something," said Tyler.

Marius spoke again, slapped some money on the bar, and got up, throwing on a jacket without a second glance backwards.

"Real charmer," said Tyler.

"There's a reason he couldn't catch a ride to the game," she said.

"When will they be back?" asked Tyler.

"Late, late tonight," said Maria.

"Too late for celebrating?" asked Tyler. "Too late to light candles in the window of the big house on the hill?"

"Yes," she said.

"So they *do* light the candles in the house," he said.

"It is done when we win," said Maria. "It means nothing else."

"So it won't hurt anything if I go up and take a look?" asked Tyler.

"You shouldn't do that."

"Why not?" he asked, teasing her.

"Because the townspeople will be pissed if they see you sticking your foreign nose into their traditions, you dummy," she said. "We are trying to protect you, believe it or not.

Most people here have no love for Americans, and you're a referee on top of it. Use your brain. Not everything is a mystery to be solved."

"I wasn't--" he started, and then she kissed him, her lips on his, and they were warm, and soft. Her tongue probed his, and he returned her kiss.

He felt her there, the golden aura surrounding them both. After the misery of his time in Krav, it was a welcome sanctuary.

Then her touch vanished, and his eyes were open again.

"You talk too much," she said. "But you're a good kisser."

"Thanks," he said, his face turning red, like he was a teenager again.

"You are very cute," she said. "What are you doing on Friday?"

"I'm reffing a game," he said.

"No, after."

"Presumably running for my life," he said.

"We will go out," she said. "I will protect you."

"Can you?"

"As much as anyone can," she said.

The night wore on. Maria continued bringing him beers, and they talked. She kissed him one more time, right before he left, a small, sweet kiss, her warm body pressed against his.

"I'll see you on Friday," she said. "Be smart during the game." Then she walked up the road, towards her modest home that lay under the shadow of the stone house on the hill, with split circles for windows and candles behind glass.

He went home, and for once, football wasn't on his mind.

8

The chant from the crowd vibrated in Tyler's bones. He could feel the song inside him. He could feel it in his blood.

It was game day again, the last few days blending together. He hadn't seen Maria since the night they kissed. The feeling kept resurfacing in his mind, and Mark's words of don't get involved.

The game superseded all of it. The season was wearing on, and each match carried more and more pressure with it. Krav could be promoted to Level 3 if it did well. Their chief competitor, Arba FC, stood even with them in points. The town buzzed with another big game.

Mark woke up Tyler early, to get to the field ahead of the crowd, same as the last time. They wore the same hoodies, drawn up tight over their heads. The overcast sky threatened cold rain. Tyler felt scattered drops as they walked over to the field, past the players warming up, into the depths of the stadium. Tyler glanced at the pitch as he passed. Its green was alive, stunning him, even on a cloudy day. The split circle called to him. He shook it off.

They could relax in the locker room. Tyler changed into his uniform, the yellow shirt and black pants, and sat, trying to focus on his breathing, even as the fans arrived and the stadium began to shake. The crowd jumped, danced, and sang in a familiar rhythm. *Krav Krav Krav.*

Mark stayed in the locker room with him this time, with no excursions out into the wild. They hadn't spoken much in the intervening days. Mark had spent little time in the apartment, and Tyler had devoted most of his to George's shop. Mark would leave as Tyler was getting home, never telling Tyler where he went. Tyler wanted to go out, maybe to Bautura, to visit Maria, but the threat of Grigore seeing him kept him inside. He was still unsure of Grigore's relationship with Maria, and he didn't want to test his temper. Better to avoid him. He'd see Maria tonight. All he had to do was get through today's game. If he could do it with his ethics intact was a different question all together.

"You ready?" asked Mark, looking at Tyler. Mark looked tired, with circles under his eyes, thin skeins of red shooting through them.

"I suppose so," said Tyler.

"I'm letting you off the leash a little bit today," said Mark.

"So I can call things now?" asked Tyler. "Actually do my job?"

"Don't be a jackass," said Mark. "Be smart about it. Don't risk our lives over an offside."

"So don't call anything, basically?" asked Tyler.

"I didn't say that," said Mark. "But yes."

"I don't know if I can do that," said Tyler.

"Don't be stupid," said Mark. "I won't be upset if you call something egregious. But if the game is out of hand, and knowing the opposing team today, it will be, swallow your whistle."

The rhythmic stomping picked up.

"It's also going to be pouring by the time the game starts, so expect a sloppy match anyway," said Mark.

"Can't they postpone it?" asked Tyler.

"They don't delay games due to weather. Maybe if someone got struck by lightning," said Mark. "Maybe. I wouldn't count on it. But I give you permission to run if Zeus starts throwing thunderbolts."

"I appreciate that," said Tyler. "How much longer until game time?"

"A half hour," said Mark. "Close your eyes and imagine Maria." He took a towel and draped it over his face.

"Jesus Christ," said Tyler. "Does nothing stay a secret in this town?"

"No, usually not,' said Mark, his voice coming from beneath the towel. "Another reason not to piss Grigore off out on the field today."

"What she does is none of his business," said Tyler.

"You're right," said Mark. "Let's see if you being right keeps his fist from so delicately reshaping your face. I told you not to get involved."

"It's not always that simple," said Tyler.

"Mate, you're preaching to the bloody choir," he said. "But keep your head on a swivel anyway. Grigore will be busy beating the snot out of Mlastina today. They have a habit of playing dirty, so it should be wonderful, watching them hurt each other."

The torrential rain soaked both Mark and Tyler as soon as they emerged onto the field. Both teams were out in it, along with Vlad, although he wore a poncho on the sidelines. Tyler caught Vlad looking at him, just like he observed the other team, and then Mark was there, speaking to Vlad. Grigore spotted him, from his spot in the split circle and walked over to Tyler. He looked down at him.

"I've heard some rumors about you, baby chick," he said.

"Can never trust the grapevine," said Tyler.

"This has nothing to do with grapes," said Grigore. "There is rumor, that you are seeing Maria."

"And?" asked Tyler.

"And I would like to know if that is true," said Grigore.

"What do you mean by seeing?" asked Tyler. Twisting him around in his words wasn't fair to Grigore in his second language, but Tyler doubted it'd change much if it was in Romanian.

"You stay away from her," said Grigore. "She is mine."

"We live a kilometer from each other," said Tyler. "I can only stay so far away. And she didn't seem too fond of you at the bar the other night."

Grigore paused. "That was love tap," he said. "And you understand me." He raised a finger and pointed it at Tyler's chest.

"Touching an official is an automatic red card," said Tyler, casually. "So I'd be careful." Grigore kept his finger there, and smiled.

"You are funny," he said. "But if I discover, baby chick,

that it is more than rumor, you will have hard time."

"Don't you have a game to worry about?" asked Tyler.

Grigore laughed, rain dashing off his forehead. "Football is like breathing. I don't think about it. I just do."

And then he walked off. Tyler looked to the crowd. The stands were full, even with the rainfall. Some wore ponchos. Most, however, endured the downfall, singing, jumping up and down, and chanting. It was louder than the last game, a crescendo towards the end of the season. The banners still hung, soaked through with water. The split circle in red bled through the white cloth. There seemed to be more of them, on longer poles, standards waving in the rain. The fans chanted as it approached game time. *Krav Krav Krav.*

Then his bones began to shake, as the chanting grew louder and louder. Grigore gestured to them, raising his arms, up and down, encouraging them. They responded with more noise. Tyler jumped as the sound of explosions filled the air. He turned to see fireworks firing off into the sky, bright sparks from first one spot, and then multiple spots throughout the crowd. Christ, he had never seen that before. Only heard of it.

The game started, and the rain poured. Mark hadn't lied. The game was hardly a game. It was mostly a fight.

Tyler thought Krav were brutes after his initial game reffing, using their size and strength to win battles for the ball. But Mlastina were that without any amount of skill or coaching. The Krav faithful drowned out the few Mlastina fans in attendance. After the first two players got dumped in the mud, Mark issued yellow cards to both. The home crowd booed thoroughly, only because the Krav player was punished as well.

Tyler saw what he was doing. Yellows now to try and control the game. Tyler recognized Krav as the better team. If they took an early lead, maybe Mlastina would lose some of its fight. Krav scored quickly after the yellow card. Grigore cut through the mud, none of Mlastina able to stop him, with a shot the goalie had no chance on.

And then Krav scored again. And again. The crowd roared after each goal, building on its previous volume, a foundation of sound that established and reestablished itself, exponentially larger and larger. Tyler tried to concentrate on the match. He watched the players, but the noise of the chant was inside him now. All he heard was *Krav Krav Krav*.

As Krav took a bigger and bigger lead, the game did not go any smoother. The Mlastina players got more and more frustrated, and used more and more underhanded tactics. Against a different team, that might have worked. It only inspired the same from Krav, and the match became a shit storm. Tyler called a yellow on a Mlastina player, who then shoved Tyler. Mark gave him an immediate red, and the crowd screamed. The rain didn't let up, and the ground grew sodden, the water the only thing capable of diminishing the impossible green of the field. Still, the mud itself seemed more vibrant, as it soaked into the earth.

Mlastina calmed down, and Krav scored several more times. Grigore strode his way around and through the slower players of the other team. He was in his element here, allowed to be the beast he was. At a certain point, Tyler swallowed his whistle. This is the game Mlastina wanted, and it was the game they got. They just weren't as good at it as Krav was.

But Grigore only fed on the lack of calls. He became more and more aggressive, using his massive frame and strength. Multiple opposing players tried to muscle the ball away from him, only to be shouldered or forearmed and fall into the muck. Both teams' uniforms were thoroughly covered now, clumps of mud caked onto arms and legs. But through all of this Grigore smiled, his white teeth gleaming in the mire.

And he only got more aggressive. His chest heaved as he pushed himself, chasing down the ball, tapping an infinite supply of energy. Mlastina, once bold with their dirty tactics, now were fading. They tried to outmaneuver him, just to keep the ball away from him for as long as possible. But it was no use. He was a man among boys. He started laughing as he played, yelling loudly in Romanian as he stole the ball, or shouldered through a small gap in men to take it from them and score. He was embarrassing them, and he was enjoying it.

"Like breathing, baby chick," he yelled at Tyler as he passed him, on the way to score again. And then he was down, one of the opposing team's players spearing him at a full sprint, a blatant tackle. Tyler was there, a red card already up, but he wasn't fast enough, because Grigore was on his feet, the spear only knocking him down, not hurting him, because nothing could hurt Grigore. The other player was picking himself off the muddy earth when Grigore punched him, once, a huge right cross across the temple, knocking the Mlastina player unconscious, dead to the world. He fell to the ground.

The crowd grew louder than ever now, their taste for blood whetted. They launched more fireworks. The chants for Krav became louder and louder. They wanted Grigore to beat him, to kill him, and Grigore could, as easy as breathing. Tyler stopped him, got in his way, and Grigore shoved him, and Tyler didn't think about it, he held up the same red card and then there was chaos.

If Tyler thought the crowd was loud before, he had heard nothing. The volume doubled, then tripled, filling the stadium, filling the town. Grigore yelled at him, enraged, but Tyler couldn't hear a word. The crowd's noise overwhelmed everything. Grigore charged, his fists tensed, and then Tyler was on the ground. But not from Grigore. From Mark.

Mark had tackled him, running over as soon as the first fight started.

"You DO NOT get up until I get you," he said, and then he was off of him, standing up in front of Grigore, waving his arms back and forth, as wide as he could, shaking his head. He was reversing the red card, literally yelling in Grigore's face. "NO CARD NO CARD NO CARD." Tyler could hear, over the din of the crowd, only quieting down so they could understand what was happening.

Mark had tempered Grigore's rage, if only a little, the opposing player just now coming to, his teammates carrying him off the field by the arms. The rain continued to pour. Mark called over both coaches, the Mlastina coach afraid to be near Grigore. Mark talked to them both, a brief conference between the three. After some spirited head movement from Mark and both the coaches, he was back at Tyler's side. Mark knelt down next to him and picked him off the ground.

"What did you do?" asked Tyler.

"Saved your fucking life, that's what I did," he said. "I

called the game due to weather, a Krav victory. The crowd doesn't know it yet, but it will in about thirty seconds. Fucking sprint to the apartment, and do not stop for anything. Lock yourself in, and I'll be along. Do not answer the door for anyone but me."

Tyler ran. Mark was right, because thirty seconds later, the fans exploded behind him.

Tyler was gone before the riot started.

9

Tyler waited in the apartment as he heard the chaos outside. The fans had learned the game ended early and they weren't happy about it. He hoped that Mark would make it back.

The minutes ticked by, as the crowd raged through the streets. They screamed and chanted, the rain and thunder still roaring, the two sounds mixing together. The noise meshed into a thundering cacophony, sounding like the damned in hell. Tyler waited.

Tyler jumped at a series of knocks at the door. He looked through the peephole, and Mark stood there, a thin line of blood running down his face from his scalp. Tyler opened it.

"Jesus, are you okay?" asked Tyler.

"I've been better," said Mark. "But I'll survive. Someone

caught me with a bottle." Mark brushed past Tyler into the apartment, grabbing some paper towels from the kitchen. He wiped away the blood from his head. He then took a dish towel, threw some ice in it, and held it to the wound.

"Can I help?" asked Tyler.

"Aye, you can help. You can fucking not pull red cards on fucking Grigore," said Mark.

"He hit the other player," said Tyler. "He pushed me. What was I supposed to do?"

"Swallow your pride and take it," said Mark. "You're not that dumb."

"Grigore was going to kill him," said Tyler. "He was unconscious. You saw Grigore's face. Am I supposed to look away while he murders a man on the field?"

"The man has teammates," said Mark. "And he speared Grigore first. Regardless of what you think of the Bear, he was defending himself. That player earned his beating."

"This isn't MMA, Mark," said Tyler. "This is football."

"Your beautiful game is a million kilometers away," said Mark. "It doesn't exist here, not in this place. What you saw out there--that's what the game is. It is a game of blood, and you're upsetting the locals. And they will make you pay if you continue. You are lucky it's raining."

"Why is that?" asked Tyler.

"Because no matter how angry they are, they'll still not want to get wet. They will go inside, warm up, remember they won, and drink some more. It'll be normal celebrating, instead of tearing your fucking guts out while they drag you from the apartment celebrating."

"This town--"

"I can't save you every time," said Mark. "You need to forget your conscience real fast, or you won't be leaving Krav."

The apartment shook with a pounding on the door.

"Don't fucking answer it," said Mark, still holding the ice on his head.

Tyler looked out the peephole.

"It's two players. From Krav. I don't remember their names."

"Let me get it," said Mark. Tyler backed up, away from the door. Mark opened it.

"Raul, Iosef," said Mark. They wore track suits, their hair wet from the rain. They were stone faced. Both stood as tall as Tyler, with broad shoulders. They looked like brothers.

They spoke in Romanian to Mark, and pointed at Tyler. Mark said something back, and they shook their heads. They pointed again and said the same again, louder.

"Looks like you're going with them, mate," said Mark, turning to Tyler.

"What for?" asked Tyler.

"Vlad wants to talk to you," said Mark. "And I'm not gonna try and stop them."

The rain had driven most of the crowd indoors, as Mark had predicted. It still poured, gutters filling with water. The drainage couldn't keep up. Tyler followed Raul and Iosef, one in front of him, the other behind, back to the field. Some stragglers wandered the streets, but some quick glances from the two large men sent them about their business.

Tyler walked quickly, his eyes naturally darting around, when he saw one. He couldn't help it. A split circle, dangling from a rooftop on the way to the stadium.

The woman was dying. She was in a bed now, a normal bed, and she was alone, alone except for Tyler. She spoke, her cadence changing, her eyes shifting. She convulsed, her body seized, and then was still. Her eyes were hers again, and she looked at Tyler with love and sadness. But she was bleeding, from her nose, her ears, her eyes, and she looked at Tyler, and then she died.

Iosef ran into Tyler, and Tyler was back. Iosef motioned for him to move, and Tyler did. He didn't know what he was seeing. Visions of a woman, living and dying. Rituals of sacrifice.

I'm losing my mind.

He barely had time to think before they had arrived. Into the stadium they went, past some chain link fences, through an entrance that Tyler hadn't seen before. A red door, painted the color of Krav.

The hallway they came upon was no different from the corridor he had seen earlier in the day. This one ran through the heart of Krav FC's offices, where the players watched tape and worked out. He hadn't seen it yet, and seemed impossible for a town the size of Krav to have. But here it was.

They led him to another red door, and opened it for him. They posted up outside as Tyler went in.

The office wasn't huge, a massive corner desk dominating the space, covered in papers, binders, and folders, all open, strewn about. Framed photos hung on the walls, all pictures of Vlad with famous footballers. Tyler recognized some of them. Some had been autographed. Trophies and signed footballs sat on every flat surface, every square bit of real estate taken up by *something*. A gigantic leather office chair sat behind the desk, tall, the seat nearly three feet off the ground. Perched in it was Vlad. He dropped what he read when he saw Tyler. He didn't stand up to greet him.

Tyler stood in the doorway, waiting.

"Sit," said Vlad, gesturing to a small chair on the other side of the desk. Tyler sat, seeing Vlad up close for the first time, with those quick, dark eyes looking right back. His plain face felt like stone. He looked down at Tyler.

"We meet, finally," said Vlad, revealing his teeth. Tyler realized this was his attempt at a smile, with no upturn on the corners of his mouth.

"Everyone was surprised that we hadn't met," said Tyler.

"I am glad to hear that I shape conversation," he said, his accent thick, but his English good. "It is expected. How are you enjoying my city?"

"It's treating me alright, so far," said Tyler. "Mark and George are getting me settled." Tyler felt a coldness from Vlad, even as he asked friendly questions.

"Mark and I go way back," said Vlad. "He understands. George as well, but we--we have a gap between us, do you understand?"

"I think so," said Tyler. "George is a little bit more blunt about describing your relationship."

"How did he describe it?"

"He said that you're destroying the town and its traditions by turning it to football," said Tyler. The same non-smile returned to Vlad's face.

"Destroying the town?" asked Vlad. "That's where he is mistaken. I'm saving it. I'm doing what is necessary to make Krav a great place. For my children, and my children's children. I leave it, to pursue my dreams, and it falls apart. It becomes forgotten. So I come back to save it. And he hates me for it."

"I think he hates you for the leaving," said Tyler. "Not the coming back."

"No, he hates me because I tried to make something with my life," said Vlad. "And George has done nothing but fix refrigerators. He hates me because I left to chase my dreams, and then when my body failed me, I came back to make a new legacy. I did more in the leaving and failing than he has done in his entire life. And now I wish to do more, and drag my city back into the sun, and he hates me. Well, let him hate me. The people understand my vision, and they support me. He should thank me. I did not throw the old ways into the garbage. I took them and made them new. Made them relevant."

"I have no dog in the fight," said Tyler.

"You say that, Mr. Tyler," said Vlad. "But then I see what happened today. And I am not so sure."

"I was doing my job," said Tyler. "Nothing more, nothing less."

"Your job was to start a riot?"

"No, my job is to enforce order," said Tyler.

Vlad laughed, a barking wheeze that winnowed away to nothing.

"Not here," he said. "Mark is not taking care of you if he hasn't told you that."

"Yeah, I know," said Tyler. "And I understand the rules here are a little different. But they still don't include letting your sociopathic striker beat an unconscious man. And he put his hands on me. I don't care if I'm reffing prison games, that's non-negotiable."

Vlad put his hands up in surrender. "The Bear is sometimes a handful. I know better than anyone," he said. "And I do my best to contain him. I don't want us to be enemies,

Mr. Tyler. I want us to be friends."

"Like Mark?"

"Yes," said Vlad. "Exactly. You understand."

"Do you know why I'm here?" asked Tyler.

"I do not," said Vlad. "It is perplexing. You don't have Drastovian blood, do you?"

"No," said Tyler. "I was friends with the wrong people. It hurt me in the end. Either I dropped football entirely, or I came here."

"And you chose Krav?"

"No, I chose football," said Tyler.

"I see," said Vlad. "I choose Krav. First as player. Then as coach. And now, mayor. The people, they rely on me. They put their trust in me. *Krav* put its trust in me. I can feel it, sometimes, when I step onto the field. When I walk on Ufranda Road. I feel the city below me, asking me to help. And to do that, I must win football games."

"Maybe patching some potholes would be a good start," said Tyler.

Any sense of that smile vanished from Vlad's face.

"Since you are not from here, Mr. Tyler, I will give you an education. Krav used to be a respectable town. A farming town. Useful to Stroescu, the Soviet puppet that he was. But as the years went on, we became less useful. And so we were forgotten by Stroescu. *Krav* was forgotten by Stroescu. And it began to fall. I was gone by then, escaped. And then Stroescu falls, and the Soviets fall back, disappear. And Drastovia has bold new leadership. New president, democracy. Very exciting. But none of this helps Krav. Krav is still forgotten. Now, ignored, left to rot and die because we represent the worst of Stroescu's time. We need the money more than anyone, and for that fact we are given nothing. I had to bend and break our money to make our field, to build a stadium. You want me to fix potholes? I need money for that, I need support. And I will get that with a team that is Level 3, Level 2, Level 1. It will bring people here, and Krav will be back in the sun."

"You think Krav can be Level 1?" asked Tyler. "That's the elite."

"I do not *think* anything, Mr. Tyler," said Vlad. "We will be, in time. And you can be a part of it. As Krav succeeds, so will you. You and Mark will be brought into the sun, right alongside. You do not need to referee for all your life. Have you ever thought to coach? As we grow, I will need real assistants, not these off-duty plumbers. And then perhaps, one day, you are head coach, for successful team. That can be you."

"That's a lot of ifs," said Tyler.

"Trust in Krav, as I have, and it will happen. But it is up to you. Your stay here can be good. Can be bad. Your decision. But please keep in mind that Krav *will* be known as a football town. I will drag it back into the sun. I will not let anything stand in my way. I will do whatever is necessary to ensure it."

10

The rain had stopped by the time Maria pulled up to the apartment in her black jeep. The town had forgotten its earlier anger. Krav enjoyed its revelry again, drinking and celebrating the win. It was still early in the evening, with no red hoods in sight.

"Aren't you losing business?" asked Tyler, as he hopped into the passenger seat of the vehicle. "Not working on the night of a home game victory?"

"I own the place. I took the night off," said Maria, with a smile. "And money isn't everything."

"Isn't that why your father moved you here? To bring more money to Krav?" he asked. Maria pulled away from the apartment building, driving back through town. Stragglers on the road, dressed in Krav red, stumbled from one place to another. They looked inside as they passed, seeing him with Maria. Tyler half ducked his head, trying to avoid their stares, but he knew it wouldn't work. If the town hadn't known about them already, they did now.

"You can't hide in Krav," said Maria. "And money doesn't matter to my father. If he wanted money, we would have stayed in London. I take it you finally talked to him?"

"More he talked to me," said Tyler. "It wasn't a pleasant conversation."

"They rarely are with my father," said Maria. "Did he mention me at all?"

They passed the statue that marked the unofficial border of Krav. Outside of town, occasional beacons from ramshackle homes served as the only light.

"He didn't," said Tyler.

"Good," she said. Their headlights cut a swath through the pitch black Drastovian road, Maria swerving at the last second to avoid potholes. Tyler grabbed onto what he could. Maria laughed.

"What are you worried about?" she asked.

"Rolling this jeep, and both of us being stranded out here with no medical attention for hours," said Tyler.

"You've got to learn to trust people, Tyler," she said.

"To be fair, this is our first date."

"Just giving you a taste," she said, and she surprised him with a kiss, taking her eyes off the road. He enjoyed it, even as the worry in his guts ached. She broke away as they hit a massive pothole at speed, the jeep shaking.

"See? It's worth it," she said. Her eyes gleamed in the darkness.

"Where are we going?" he asked.

"Not much farther," she said. "It is where I go when I want to get away from Krav."

They drove for a few minutes more in the dark, when she slowed down and turned onto a dirt driveway which weaved back into the hills. Sparse trees lined the road. It suddenly felt very ominous. It reminded Tyler of his vulnerability in Drastovia.

"This place feels like a horror movie," he said. "You're not planning on killing me, right?"

Maria laughed. "If I wanted to kill you, I'd do it in town. No one would stop me. Doing it out here is more work."

Maria expertly drove the Jeep down the mile-long driveway, avoiding the deep divots and ruts. Tyler bounced up and down as they moved. The bobbing headlights served as the only light for miles around. They lit the road ahead, and soon they came to a stop. The headlights revealed a decrepit shack, half fallen down, with broken windows and a destroyed roof. Maria killed the engine, and it was silent. She turned off the headlights, and they sat in darkness.

Maria got out and Tyler followed. His eyes slowly adjusted to the darkness, their footfalls loud on the packed dirt. After a minute, he could see well enough, the moon and stars giving him light. Maria had moved ahead of him already, walking around the small broken-down house toward the backyard.

The sparse trees that had lined the driveway were still here, but away from the house, giving it a little space. Weeds and scrubs had overtaken what used to be the front yard, and the faint outlines of a battered wreck of a truck stood out at the edge of his vision. The distant sound of insects surrounded them.

"You coming?" asked Maria, making him jump slightly. He followed her voice around the house, a small worn path showing the way. It led to the backyard. Time had exposed the innards of the house, with the entire back of the home fallen away. The floorboards had rotted, with weeds springing up from beneath. He could see the remnants of the kitchen and the living room. An old television sat inside, its screen broken.

Maria was sitting on a bench in the tiny backyard. A small, newer patio table stood in front of it.

"Did you put this back here?" he asked.

"I needed somewhere to sit," she said. "It will not break. Sit next to me. Keep me warm." He didn't need another invitation. He moved close to her and wrapped his arm around her. It wasn't too cold, until the wind would whip through them and they would momentarily freeze. She nestled into him. It felt good. Tyler looked out from the bench and understood why she visited this spot.

A vista laid out before them, undulating plains sinking into a valley, filled with dozens of small pools, each surrounded by copses of the same trees as around the house. The water glowed under the moon, reflecting the light. Tyler could see the stars in the water. The ponds mirrored the sky, each capturing the thousand pinpricks of light filtered down to them from millions of miles away.

"It's amazing," he said.

"This was where my father grew up," she said.

"He saw this every night?" he asked.

"More or less," she said. "Perhaps some nights there was less moon than others. But this was where he lived. Where his mother and father raised him. Where he first touched a football."

"I understand why this is where you go to get away."

"This is the first place he showed me, after we returned. I was resistant. I wanted to stay in London. I wanted *us* to stay in London. He thought his career was over, with both his knees hurt, but he still had a lot of opportunities. I was young. Petulant. I wasn't wrong, but I had never seen this. I thought Krav a backwater hole that the best people escape and never look back. I drilled this into my father, day after day, as we prepared to leave, as we traveled. I told him this was a mistake. That we were leaving the security and comfort of the big city for this forgotten town, that he was chasing for nostalgia's sake."

"This changed your mind?" he asked.

"No," she said. "But it made me understand. My father grew up here, this view the first and last thing he saw every single day. *This* is Krav to him. He had nothing but a football, and he carved a sense of pride into Krav with it as a young man. And despite that pride, the town was deprived and forgotten. And he left. But I don't think he ever forgot it. He never forgot this view. He never forgot waking up on a cold morning and dribbling the football up and down the driveway, until dust covered his legs up to the knee, his feet layered with calloused blisters. He bled into the soil, and it brought Krav pride. He wanted to do it again."

"But do you?" asked Tyler.

"I don't know," she said. "He's all I have, and I'd do anything for him. For Krav? I don't know."

"Seems a little slow for you," he said.

"Ha!" said Maria. "Slow is not the word. Glacial is better. But perhaps slow isn't terrible. Perhaps slow is better for me in the long run. And I want to see him happy."

"Would you leave without him?" asked Tyler.

"Are you planning on taking me away?" asked Maria.

"I'm just curious," said Tyler. She side-eyed him.

"I am not wed to Krav," she said. "But I will not abandon my father over minor quibbles."

"Minor quibbles like Grigore?" asked Tyler.

"Grigore is nothing to me," said Maria.

"He threatened me today," said Tyler.

"That sounds like him."

"He threatened me over you. Said he heard rumors about us, and if they were true, that I would face trouble."

Maria sighed.

"We go on one date and he thinks I'm his property," she said.

"You went on a date with him?!?" asked Tyler. "He's a monster!"

"I did not know any better at the time," she said. "There are certainly not a lot of desirable bachelors in Krav. Most are dull, ugly, or stupid. Grigore does have a certain animal magnetism--"

"Also he's controlling, and he has a temper, and he's a brute that beats men in the street for spilling drinks on them."

"--it was a single date, to be clear. We didn't even kiss. We barely touched. He continues to think he owns me."

"And your father doesn't disabuse him of that notion?" asked Tyler.

"My father doesn't care as long as he shows up for games and plays well. It is sometimes difficult enough to make him do that. The police can look away from only so much."

"That's comforting," said Tyler. "Mark told me the crowd would cheer if he killed me on the pitch."

"They probably would," said Maria. "That's different. Everything is different when a game is involved."

"I'll have to disagree, considering it's my life," said Tyler.

"It is *their* life," said Maria. "They know the stakes. It's why they voted for my father. They have pride in their town again, in themselves again. Any threat to that pride will be taken seriously. They want our town to have money and power. But they really want respect. My father gives them that. Grigore and Krav FC gives them that."

"What about the old ways?" asked Tyler. "You don't think it's exploitative to twist these peoples' beliefs around?"

"You've been eating too many of George's dumplings," said Maria.

"He makes sense," said Tyler.

"I like George," said Maria. "But he is the exception. You see the crowd. You see the town. The old ways were about pride, about taking care of Krav, of believing in her power. They are the same, and my father realized that. George would be better off accepting that, and letting bygones be bygones between him and my father. They were close, before my father left. They shared similar goals and beliefs about the town."

"But your father left," said Tyler. "And George didn't."

"George is jealous," said Maria. "And he won't admit it. He is a fine man, but he is not a leader. And that's what it took to make Krav worthy again."

"Your father suggested that if I played ball, he would give me a coaching job," said Tyler.

"I'm sure he would," said Maria. "Would it be so bad?"

"Which? Playing ball? Or staying in Krav?" he asked.

"Either," said Maria.

"I can only go so far," said Tyler.

"Ah, like action hero," said Maria, nudging him with an elbow.

"I'm serious. Bend my ethics, bend the rules only so much, before I can't take anymore. Mark doesn't care, as long as there is a modicum of rule to the games. He's tried to tell me it's in everyone's best interest in turning a blind eye...but I can't. I couldn't live with myself."

He could see the gleam of Maria's eyes in the dim, studying him. He couldn't decipher the look on her face. Confusion? Respect? Or something else?

She kissed him then, moving in slow, her body against his. He kissed back, their mouths open, and she straddled him. His hands were down her back, over her hips and ass and they kissed harder now, their mouths open wider and wider. She grinded onto him, her hips softly gyrating under his hands. Her hands were in his hair. The cold wind rushed past them but Tyler didn't notice.

Her touch was intoxicating, and there was nothing in his mind but her. His body and mind were hers.

And then she was off of him, pulling him up, back to the jeep. She drove then, with Maria turning up the radio, 80s rock as loud as it could go. She went faster, swerving more and more, but Tyler couldn't see the road anymore, watching her in the dim light. The long drive out into the country passed by much quicker on the return trip. In a flash, they were at Maria's home. She parked and they were out, and she had him by the hand, drawing him out of the vehicle, toward the house.

She unlocked the door and went inside.

He stepped onto the front porch, and then the chanting broke the reverie she had cast on him. He looked over to the stone house that overlooked the town and her home. The road snaked to it, up and around the hill, to the spot where it stood, carved into the hillside. The candles flickered in the windows. Tyler saw the split circle illuminated in each window. The flames flashed there, strong, and then his eyes went to the source of the hymn. The procession had started.

The townsfolk had gathered, dressed in the same red robes, with their faces hooded in shadow. They walked down the snaking road. Calloused hands held the white banners high, with the split circle painted in crimson, dried off from the day's rain. The mass would be there soon, and a feeling in his gut told him to stay, follow them, and see what they did. Or to sneak up into the stone house and find out the truth of what it contained.

"Are you coming?" asked Maria from inside, and her voice broke the spell. He looked in, and she stood there, naked, her clothes in a pile on the floor.

He went in, his desire for her winning out, shutting the door behind him. A minute later, the procession walked by, their chants filling the town. Tyler didn't hear it.

11

Tyler woke up the next morning naked, beside Maria in her soft, giant bed. She was draped over him, and he glanced at his phone. *Shit*. Already an hour late to work. George would be pissed.

He tried to extricate himself from under Maria without waking her up, but her eyes fluttered as she saw him move. She smiled, sleepily.

"I need to get to work," he said.

"Do you?" she asked, and pulled herself on top of him, kissing.

Tyler opened the door to George's shop just over two hours later, finding George with his head in the back of a washing machine. His greasy hands struggled with a wrench.

"I'm sorry for being late--" said Tyler.

"I see you're already picking up bad habits from Maria," said George, without looking up. "Start organizing the fasteners in those bins." He pointed to a far corner of the shop. Tyler went over and started working.

"Are there any secrets in this town?" asked Tyler.

"Of course," said George. "There are many. But you are not good at sneaking. And Maria, well, she is Maria. She does not do things quietly. Did you expect to go out with the mayor's daughter, to enter into her home, and not have anyone know?"

"We're both adults--"

"Whoa whoa whoa," said George, finally showing his face, facing Tyler, dropping the wrench onto a shop towel. "Maria is a nice girl, and you are dumb American, but I have no problem with it. Grigore, on the other hand, will hit you until you reconsider your decisions."

"I'm well aware," said Tyler.

"And you still went out with her?" asked George. "Have you never been punched before? It hurts a lot. Especially from someone who is big and strong, bigger than you."

"I try and avoid the punching as much as possible," said Tyler. "Diplomacy, and all that."

"I do not think that will work on Grigore," said George. He returned to the washing machine.

"No, he doesn't seem like the talking type," said Tyler.

"Maria will protect you," said George. "She likes you."

"What makes you say that?" asked Tyler.

"You are different from the others," said George. "You are special. I can see it in her when she speaks of you."

"You gossip," said Tyler.

"Do you think I only fix refrigerators?" asked George. "I have social life. I talk to people."

"No, I'm not an idiot," said Tyler. "You also fix washing machines."

A noise erupted from the machine, and Tyler realized it was laughter.

"Some washing machines, but not this one," said George, pulling his head back out. He dropped the wrench again. "It is stubborn bastard. Maybe he will loosen up later."

Tyler sorted the fasteners, dropping like bolts and nuts in similar plastic tubs and cardboard boxes. His hands got greasier by the moment while George wandered through the shop, moving things about, not really working. He seemed flighty today, for whatever reason. Soon it was lunchtime.

"Time to eat," said George. They had settled into a comfortable routine, of George bringing lunch for both of them, and Tyler gladly eating it. He had tried to insist to George multiple times that it wasn't necessary but George would hear nothing of it. George liked to cook and provide food, he said. So Tyler ate. Today it was sandwiches, with homemade rolls and fresh deli cut meat and cheese, with thick layers of some garlic mayonnaise that Tyler guessed George also made at home. Tyler could smell them before George even opened the paper bags. The mixture of smells made Tyler's stomach grumble. He hadn't eaten since before his date with Maria.

He took a bite and again, it was incredible. George was a magician.

"Good?" asked George. He would ask everyday, his eyes glancing at Tyler, with some deep-seated worry behind them, looking for Tyler's approval.

"It's great," said Tyler. The food would change, but the drink would always be the same tea. Not that it bothered Tyler. It was perfect. The previous day's rain clouds were long gone, with the sun out again on the cool day.

Tyler suspected George, despite his sometimes gruff exterior, just liked the company. Someone he could lecture about the state of the world, of Drastovia, of Krav. Today, it was about the parks.

"There used to be beautiful parks, all throughout the town. Green grass, playgrounds, places for children to play, for the town to congregate. Now they are gone. Gone!"

"Where did they go?" asked Tyler, the question George wanted to hear.

"They were walled off," said George, holding his glass of tea, never drinking it because he was too busy talking. "Because there's no one to mind them. Because there is no money."

"Because it was spent on Krav FC," said Tyler.

"Because it was spent on Krav FC," said George. "On that damnable stadium, instead of fields where our poor children could play that damnable sport. And now they play in the dirt. That was what Stroescu did. He built monuments to dead men in our grass, and then walled them off, and left our children in the dirt. Lament our current government as much as you want, but they didn't take the parks away from the children. Now they are abandoned again, to overgrow, to fall apart. But it does not matter to Vlad, it does not matter to the town. They will let him throw our children into the dirt so that their beloved Krav FC has a place to shame the old ways."

"There were hundreds marching last night," said Tyler.

"Just because there are many of them doesn't mean they are right," said George. He finally took a drink of tea and a bite of food. He chewed through it with no change of expression, showing no affect or appreciation for the delicious sandwich.

"What's the difference, at the end of the day?" asked Tyler. "If they still march for Krav?"

"It is not for Krav. It is for Krav FC," said George. "Those are two very different things. Just because they both use the name of Krav, does not mean they are the same."

"What's the difference?" asked Tyler. "I don't like Vlad, but I do think he wants the best for Krav in the end."

"He wants the best for Krav FC," said George. "And *he* gets to decide what that means. He defines Krav FC. He shapes it. And by linking the town and the club, he also defines what Krav is to everyone. When they think of Krav, they think of football. They do not think of the people. The people here, they do not have pride in the town, in the schools, in the parks. They have pride in football, in sport. That matters. Because then Vlad controls everything. And I don't trust him."

"Because he left?" asked Tyler.

"Yes, because he left," said George. "And regardless of what he says, or what Maria says, nothing about his return was brave, or selfless. He left as soon as he could, and only returned when he had no other options. And now that he is here, he is turning my beloved home into the only thing he has ever cared about. Football."

"Fair enough," said Tyler. "You never told me exactly what the 'old ways' are."

George swallowed what remained of the sandwich and

glanced at Tyler, not answering immediately. He breathed deeply and sighed.

"I cannot talk plainly about it," said George. "It would not make sense to you. You are an outsider. You would not understand."

"Try me," said Tyler.

George shook his head. "It is not my place to tell you. I am not the steward anymore. There are rules, rules set down long ago, and I will not break them, even if it is in my own interests."

"The steward?" asked Tyler. "Of the old ways?"

"Yes," said George. "I don't make those decisions. It was taken from me."

"Then who is?" asked Tyler.

"I don't know," said George. "I would guess Vlad. But it could be anyone. They decided after I left. They forced my hand. Now they are unrecognizable."

"I don't understand," said Tyler. "Who's they?"

"I've already said too much," said George. Tyler couldn't read him.

George took another long drink.

"What happens in the big stone house on the hill?" asked Tyler. "Is that where they make those decisions?"

"You shouldn't involve yourself, Tyler," said George, now looking him in the eye. "It is not your battle."

"I look up at it," said Tyler. "And I feel like I'm losing control." A subtle shift washed over George's face. Tyler recognized it, but couldn't identify it. "The procession, after every home game, starts there. The candles are burning in the windows. Maria won't tell me what it's in there."

"The stone house is old," said George. "Older than me.

Older than Krav itself. It was here when my family arrived. It has always been there. It is--an anchor. It holds Krav to the map."

"Have you been inside?" asked Tyler.

"Many times," said George. "Many times. It was home to me, once. It's a symbol, Tyler. A very important one, and another thing that was taken away from me by him."

George believed what he said. Tyler could see that clearly. But he remembered the feeling that house gave him. The split circle, and it's effect on his mind. He needed to see inside. He needed to know the root of it all.

"What is Krav to you, then?" asked Tyler.

"Krav is the earth here. It is the people here, who care about each other, who would fight and die for their neighbor, for their children. It is the hills, the trees, the flowers. It is about taking care of each other. It is feeding each other. It is about empathy, not supremacy."

"Football isn't about supremacy," said Tyler.

"I know you are a believer," said George. "And I know better than to argue with a believer. It will get me nowhere. But you saw how Krav FC plays. They want to dominate. *Vlad* wants to dominate."

"But that's sports," said Tyler. "And there are plenty of places with bad teams that still have pride in their home. And lots of people who play football have empathy."

"You are a believer," said George. "And you want to see the good. Be careful, that as you grow closer to Maria, that you do not also grow closer to Vlad."

"So I shouldn't trust anyone?" asked Tyler. "Maria, Mark, Vlad--is there anyone I'm forgetting?"

"Me," said George.

"Above everything else, you seem like an honest guy."

"Ha, that is where I tricked you," said George. "I plied you with dumplings and sandwiches, and you have fallen directly into my trap."

Tyler laughed, and George only smiled, a crooked display of teeth that had taken Tyler a while to recognize. They finished lunch, and went back to work. George resumed lecturing about parks and public funding and public trust while Tyler sorted bolts. Despite their conversation about the stone house and Krav, Tyler's mind instead returned again and again to Maria. Could there be a future with her in Krav? Or even in general?

It's been one date, Tyler. Take a breath or two.

But she inspired that in him. And as soon as George closed up shop, he didn't go back to his apartment. Instead he returned to her home. He could feel the stone house above him as he walked onto the porch, but Tyler fixed his gaze on the street. He knocked on her door. He had said he'd be back for dinner that night, but he didn't know if she had taken him seriously or not. When she opened it, she was in yoga pants and a t-shirt, and the smell of something delicious hit him.

She pulled him in and kissed him deeply, and he returned it. His hands slid around her, and pushed her inside, kicking the door shut behind him. The house was two stories, but relatively narrow, with a living room on the left, the kitchen on the right, with the first floor bathroom in the back. Her bedroom, a second bathroom, and a small office were upstairs.

"Dinner first," she said, gently pushing him away. "You came back. I'm glad."

"Of course I did," said Tyler. "Going home to Mark or coming here isn't much of a choice."

"You know just how to flatter me," she said, walking into the kitchen. He followed her.

"It's just pasta and salad," she said. "I hope that's okay."

"What is that smell?" he asked. "It's amazing."

"It's the sauce," she said. "Should be ready in twenty minutes or so. What did George complain about today?"

"Parks," said Tyler. "He complained that Krav doesn't have enough parks for children to play in."

"He's right," said Maria. Tyler sat down in a wooden chair at the small kitchen table, enough room for two. She stood, her back to him, stirring her sauce.

"That's what worries me," said Tyler.

"Why is that?"

"Because if he's right, and he's against your father, what does that say about your father?"

"There is room for shades of gray," she said. "I already told you, they are more similar than they'd like to admit. They both see the problems. They just have different solutions. Doesn't make either of them right or wrong. But the people back my father. I still like George, even with his complaining."

"He likes you," said Tyler. "And he knew about us, this morning, without me saying a word."

"Is there an us?" she asked, turning to face him, steam rising behind her from the stove top.

"That's a good question. Is there?"

She looked at him. She cracked a small smile, narrowing her eyes.

"There's *something*," she said. She turned back, the matter apparently settled.

"There are very few secrets in Krav," she said. "He probably told you as much."

"Except what happens in that damn house," said Tyler. "And why the town dresses up like cultists and marches through the streets after home games."

"Some things are better left secrets," she said. "Stick around long enough, and you'll find out."

"One day, you're going to tell me," he said.

"One day, I will," she said. "Are you ready to eat?"

"I'm starving," said Tyler.

She served, giving them both bowls of pasta and soup, ladling her homemade cream sauce over the pasta. It smelled amazing. He took a bite, and then the front door rattled as someone pounded on it. Maria got up and peeked through the window.

"It's Grigore," she said, walking back to the kitchen. "Ignore it." The door shuddered again, and then his voice could be heard as he shouted outside, a long string of angry Romanian. It shook again. Grigore wasn't going away.

"He'll run out of patience and leave," said Maria, and then the door flew open, Grigore's massive boot destroying the small lock. He was furious, and made a bee line for Tyler. Tyler stood up, balling his fists, ready for a fight.

Maria stepped in front of him, talking to Grigore in Romanian, but Grigore heard none of it. He swept her aside with an arm without a thought. She continued to talk, louder and louder. The distance closed between them and Grigore reached out with deceptive speed and grabbed Tyler by the collar. Tyler realized just how outmatched he was.

He had recognized Grigore's strength and quickness,

and realized he was a dangerous man, but not until this moment did he understand that in a straight up fight, he had no chance against Grigore. Grigore cocked back a massive fist, and was about to bring it down through his face. Maria continued to speak, with her voice rising until she was yelling next to them, and it didn't matter, and Tyler braced himself, and then she spoke and Grigore paused.

His face changed, from utter rage, which Tyler recognized, to a look that he couldn't place. After a few moments, he realized what it was. It was fear, something he hadn't thought Grigore capable of.

Grigore spoke to Maria out of the side of his mouth, still staring at Tyler. She answered, repeating the same phrase. Tyler knew almost no Romanian aside from a few words that Mark had taught him on his first day.

He let go of Tyler, turning all of his attention to her. Despite their size difference, Grigore seemed meek now, kowtowing to her as they went back and forth, their voices quiet, her louder than him. He asked a solitary question, and she replied strongly, and he winced.

Grigore.

Winced.

She spoke for another minute, all her attention on Grigore. Maria only stared down Grigore, who had by now bowed his head, staring at the floor. She pointed at the door. Grigore looked over at Tyler, his eyes not full of anger or rage, but of resentment and jealousy. He turned and walked out awkwardly placing the door back in frame. It would need repair.

Maria sighed, shaking her head. She sat down again.

"Are you going to eat, or not?" she asked, staring at Tyler, who still stood. He slid into his chair, shocked.

"What did you say to him?" he asked.

"I--" she started. "I convinced him who had the real power in Krav."

"Holy shit," he said.

"How's the pasta?" she asked. He took a bite, quickly.

"It's great," he said, only half-tasting it.

They finished dinner, and ended up on the couch, but there was no hiding what they both wanted. They moved into her bedroom, tearing each other's clothes off.

12

Loud knocking on the front door woke Tyler up. But it wasn't Grigore. It was Mark.

His voice filled the house.

"Sorry to intrude, but we got a fucking football game to referee," said Mark, yelling upstairs. "Put your dick away and get downstairs."

Tyler blinked his eyes awake and forced himself up. Maria awoke next to him, drowsy.

"You heard him," she said. "You've got work to do. Good luck today." He leaned down and kissed her before scrambling out of bed, throwing clothes on, and hurrying down to Mark. He stood there waiting in front of the door, still half broken.

"About fucking time," said Mark. "We're going to be late."

"I'll call father," said Maria, a sheet draped around her, standing at the top of the stairs. "I'm sure he won't mind."

"I'm sure," said Mark. "Did you know your door is broken? Not very safe. Anyone could just barge right in here."

"So observant," she said. "No wonder you're such a good referee. You see everything." Mark fake smiled and turned to Tyler, ushering him outside.

"I've got your gear," said Mark. "Throw on the hoodie. We've need to move."

"I'm sorry. I lost track," said Tyler.

"She has that effect," said Mark. "I told you, I told you--"

"Yes, I know," said Tyler. "Don't get involved."

Mark walked quickly. The sun shone brightly with no worries about rain. Fans already filled the street, walking towards the arena. Today was different. There were more people, more visitors. They all wore bright green and black. Tyler hustled to keep up with Mark.

"Lots of opposing fans out today," said Tyler. Mark kept hurrying, his head down. He seemed tense, tenser than usual. "You okay?"

"No, I am not o-fucking-kay," said Mark. "I am worried, and I'd appreciate you taking some of that burden if you could."

"What's wrong?" asked Tyler.

"Krav is playing Arba today," said Mark.

"They're green and black?" asked Tyler.

"Sherlock Holmes is going to be asking you for advice on his next murder," said Mark. "Yes, their colors are green and black. And they have a dynamite team."

"You're worried Krav might lose?" asked Tyler.

"No," said Mark. "Krav is *going* to lose. I'm worried that

someone might bash my fucking head in *after* they lose."

"Arba's that good?"

"Yes," said Mark. "They have suffered a precipitous fall the past few seasons, but they were Level 2 just three years ago."

"And now they're down here?" asked Tyler. "Jesus, what happened?"

"Half the team died in a bus accident," said Mark. "It'll put a damper on a team's future."

"Christ," said Tyler.

"Yes, but they've bounced back. The half that survived developed, and they've poached a bunch of good players. And not Level 4 good, but actually good. They are neck and neck with Krav for promotion. And I don't think Krav can do it, not today."

"Nothing a few bent rules can't fix?" asked Tyler.

"No," said Mark. "Keep your head on a swivel."

Tyler felt the difference in the air. The Krav faithful still filled the stands with their banners waving. But their chants sounded less raucous, a little unsure. Their faith would be tested today.

They got to their locker room with just enough time to change. No moments of reflection or concentration today. Tyler changed into his gear and laced his cleats quickly. Mark changed beside him. Away from Maria, the normal game day anxiety returned, the unease building up inside his guts. The fever dream confrontation with Grigore last night popped into his mind, and the anxiety doubled. Grigore would be out there, and Maria wouldn't be there to call off the rabid bear.

Mark tapped him on the shoulder, gesturing to the door.

"Let's go face it," said Mark, and they were winding through the halls, out onto the vibrant field of Krav.

The field exploded into Tyler's vision. Logic told him that the rain from the previous week had rejuvenated the tired grass, and gave it new life, the bold emerald almost Technicolor, searing itself onto his retina, seeing green even when he looked away, the bright white lines still there when he closed his eyes.

The split circle.

It was the rain. That's all it was.

But inside, he knew, knew it wasn't just that. He looked to the crowd, and they packed the bleachers, like always. The fans waved their banners, covered in red. Everyone stood singing. The Arba fans were largely segregated, but still a sizable crowd, much more than any other fan base he had seen yet. They occupied a corner of one side, standing and chanting their own songs. Tyler knew the Krav songs, knew their rhythm and refrains. The Arba song felt wrong.

Tyler had misdiagnosed the unsaid worry from the Krav fans on the walk to the arena. They were worried, of course they worried, but their faith was strong. He could feel it bombarding him as they sang, as they chanted, as they waved their scarves and banners. Krav had carved a path through the season, and had strengthened the faith of their followers.

And it fed the grass. Their belief kept it bright.

The memory of last night, of Grigore, popped into his mind once again. He scanned the field for him, finding him quickly. He was doing his normal warm-up. He jumped up and down, gesturing wildly toward the crowd, whipping them into a frenzy. They began to cheer louder and louder for him and for Krav. Grigore didn't once glance in his direction. Maria had put the fear of God into him, somehow.

Vlad was there as well, but all of his attention was on Arba. Tyler doubted that Vlad was in the dark about him and Maria, but he didn't seem to care about it too much at the moment.

The opposing team warmed up on their side of the field, sprinting and stretching. None of them approached the size of Grigore, or even the other larger members of Krav, but they were quick. They cut in and out of drills, passing back and forth. As he scanned their faces, they didn't study the fans, or even the Krav players. They looked unconcerned.

Game time approached rapidly, and the crowd got louder and louder. The stands shook. The game started, and Mark was right. Arba was very good.

Mark had made the point to him early on about how Vlad understood how Level 4 worked. Vlad had assembled a team built around size. Grigore and his team of brutes were fast, but most other teams in the division simply couldn't handle how big they were. Most of the players at this level worked full-time jobs doing something else. Most were school teachers or plumbers or some other menial job. Krav set itself apart just having athletes like Grigore, full-time footballers.

Arba had them as well, and they weren't as big as Krav. But they were *fast*. And Krav couldn't keep up.

Arba took control quickly, keeping possession for most of the first period, scoring twice. The score belied how clear the talent disparity on the field was. Arba danced around Krav at will, the Krav players trying their usual tricks but failing. The physical play didn't work on them. Grigore played hard. His chest heaved with exertion as he sprinted up and down the field. His egging on of the crowd disappeared after the game started because he was too tired, his big body getting worn out. The Arba coach had scouted well and knew how to use the size of Krav against them. All of Krav's players were fit, but they hadn't been tested like this. The Arba players kept their heads and eyes up, and any time a Krav player tried to hip check them, to tangle up their legs, they danced away, making the attacking Krav player look foolish.

Arba attacked the Krav goal over and over again. The Krav keeper kept them in the game. He played out of his mind. Grass stains covered him by intermission, his body sliding all over the goal to keep the ball out.

Tyler didn't need to swallow his whistle, because Arba's ability nullified any of the normal penalties Krav would have committed. Mark called a few questionable offsides penalties against Arba, but it did no good. They would simply reclaim possession and carry on. They didn't go after Mark, or him.

Krav retreated to the locker room at intermission, covered in sweat and looking beaten. Tyler looked up at the crowd, and the worry was evident now, palpable. The deficit had subdued the familiar chants and singing, with a few banners held down. The faithful strength to hold them aloft throughout the entire game had disappeared.

"Okay," said Mark, alone with Tyler at intermission. "Escape plan. If we have a clear shot, we sprint directly to the apartment, hole up there. If we're penned in, we head to our locker room and deadbolt the door."

"This is clearly not our fault," said Tyler.

"Doesn't matter, mate," said Mark. "With so many opposing fans here, we'll be a more attractive target than even the other team."

"Why?" asked Tyler.

"No protection," said Mark. "The fans that travel want to scrap. Hard as nails."

Mark's earlier worries turned out true as the second half started, with Krav walking out of the locker down 2-0. Arba had outclassed them. But Krav didn't give up. Because Vlad had a plan.

Arba had put their most skilled defensive player on Grigore. He was quick, and agile, and tired Grigore out, making him work twice as hard to get and maintain possession. Any time Grigore tried to use his size, the Arba player danced away, out of reach. Grigore was powerless and frustrated, and it forced him into bad decisions. But Krav had figured out a way to free Grigore over the break.

By knocking Grigore's pest out of the game.

Iosef, one of the two brutes that had escorted Tyler to Vlad's office, did it. As soon as the second half started, he charged the pest and hit him as hard as he could, blindsiding and then landing on him, driving him into the ground. The crowd roared in reaction, both fan bases screaming. Mark was right there, ready, almost too ready, with a red card for Iosef. The Krav fans screamed again, for blood, but Iosef only stood up, brushing the dirt off of him. He smiled and walked off the pitch. Vlad turned to the fans and held up a single finger, and the crowd's anger dissipated, if only a little. All part of the plan, he was telling them, and they understood. A medic had hustled out to the Arba player, giving them smelling salts, bringing them back around. Their arm hung limply at the shoulder, and they marched off the field, still woozy.

Vlad had traded one of his disposable hammers for Arba's best defensive player, to free his best striker.

And it worked.

Arba played differently after that moment. They play scared, still dancing, but franticly, knowing there could be a giant bearing down on them from behind at any point. And it freed Grigore to attack, finally getting and keeping possession. He marched up and down the field, and after a few strong chances, scored. In the thralls of a barbarous frenzy, he ran along the crowd's edge, ripping off his top and windmilling it around his head. The home crowd responded in kind. They screamed and roared, the chants of Krav growing louder and louder. Tyler could feel the pressure of the hymns. They surrounded him. Disorientation hit him and waves of confusion and sickness washed over him. His stomach roiled, and images flashed in his closed eyes.

The split circle.

The stone house.

Maria.

And then it was gone, and he could breathe again. The nausea had vanished, as quick as it arrived, and he felt normal again. They resumed play after the goal, the entirety of Krav screaming at the top of their lungs, all the Krav players ready to go. It looked as if Krav had regained the momentum and demonstrated how Vlad would drag them back into the sun. Arba would collapse.

Except they didn't. Arba fought through the wave of Krav momentum, and the game entered a stalemate, both challenging for goals, neither scoring. Mark blew a few more whistles on Arba, but it did nothing to help Krav. They couldn't score. Grigore did his best to will the ball into the goal, but Arba swarmed him, and Krav did not have the depth that Arba had.

Sweat covered Tyler as he ran up and down the field. The crowd's tension only built, as the remaining time in the half ran out. They needed a goal to tie, and a tie would satisfy them. It would have to, against Arba. A draw would give them a strong chance toward promotion. A loss would make it difficult, forcing a victory against Arba in their second match, later in the season.

Krav was desperate, and made some mistakes out of that desperation. Their goalie kept them in the game, stopping several high danger chances from Arba, but time was running out. Regulation play ended, but Mark added on stoppage time. Tyler caught the harried glance from Vlad to Mark beforehand. Mark was doing all in his power to give Krav a chance.

And they took it. With stoppage time adding up, Grigore took possession and passed ahead to a cutting striker, and who then sprinted while he juked defenders. He passed back to Grigore, closer to the net now. Arba squeezed on him, the nearest four players rushing towards him. He was Krav's best player and pressuring him had worked all day.

Tyler saw the whole play. Grigore had a moment to shoot. It was a hard shot, not impossible, but unlikely to go in. Arba had pressured him into bad shots all game, and so Grigore passed, back to the other Krav player, whose name Tyler knew was Dario. It was a difficult pass, harder than the shot, Tyler would have reckoned. But it made it through traffic, right at his feet, and Dario was wide open then, only the net in front of him. The noise of the crowd was over-whelming, a great ocean waiting to crash. He reared back, and shot.

He missed and the ball sailed wide left, out of bounds. The crowd collapsed, the sound of a gut being punched. Arba took the ball then, and moved it down the field, and Mark called it, had to, he couldn't let stoppage run forever.

Krav lost.

Everything exploded, all at once.

13

The arena exploded into chaos. The "riot" at the end of the rain game was nothing. This was madness, and all Tyler could do was run. But he stayed frozen as the crowd was pouring out of the stands onto the field.

The Arba fans stuck together as a group, running toward their team. Arba FC had retreated, hoping to leave through one of the exits and get to their locker room or bus. The Arba fans surrounded them, protecting them. The Krav fans outnumbered them, and they were lashing out at anything and everything, taking the path of least resistance.

Their faith had been rewarded with a loss, and righteous anger fueled them as they raged. With the Arba team protected, they were attacking anything that moved. Some had already fled the arena, either to hide from the horde or to sow destruction elsewhere. Vlad was nowhere to be seen, having retreated to the safety of his office. Most of the Krav players had also run, aside from Grigore. He reveled in the chaos, clotheslining anyone who got close to him, roaring the entire time. His hammerhead grin flashed with every blow.

"Wake the *fuck* up, Tyler," said Mark, who sprinted at him and grabbed his arm as he went. "They'll realize pretty quick that we're easy targets. Hurry. To the locker room."

Mark was right. A brief glance saw a cluster of angry people rushing towards them, realizing the refs were vulnerable. They ran.

The group of Krav fans chasing them gained members as they sprinted across the field. Tyler and Mark rushed toward the access door to the innards of the arena. Tyler forced his weary legs forward, even after the exhaustion of the game. A sharp bolt of pain erupted from his head and he stumbled. He almost fell, but Mark caught him and they continued to run. Tyler reached to his scalp, his hand coming back covered in blood. He'd have to worry about it later. A bottle flew by him, and then he would swear he heard the sound of a whip behind him. Tyler glanced back, and sure enough, a Krav fan carried a whip, his face covered in rage.

They weaved and dodged through other fans, all running to different places, the arena full of confusion. They reached the access door, and sprinted down the hallways, Mark ahead of Tyler, the crowd on their heels.

The fans yelled as they ran, phrases of angry Romanian hurled at them. Tyler didn't know what they meant, but he understood them. They needed someone to blame. Something to pin the loss on. They had done everything right.

They had paid for their devotion, for their faith, and they had still lost. Someone must be to blame. It couldn't be Krav's fault.

They gained on Mark and Tyler. Their second wind waned, their tired legs catching up to them. But the door was there, to their locker room, and they were through it, Mark first, then Tyler, Mark's desperate eyes on him as he slammed it closed right after him, holding it shut and engaging three sets of deadbolts.

The thick metal door shook as angry fists battered it. Mark tentatively let go, and it held. There was nothing the fans had that could get through, even as the banging continued.

"Jesus," said Mark. "That was too close."

"I've never seen anything like that," said Tyler.

"Stay in Krav long enough," said Mark. "And you'll see worse."

The thumping stopped after a few minutes. The crowd moved on, looking for an easier target. Still, Mark and Tyler waited, changing back into their street clothes.

"We give 'em half an hour," said Mark. "Give them a chance to spread out their chaos a little bit. Then we go to the apartment and keep our heads down."

"I don't know why they were attacking us," said Tyler. His head had stopped bleeding, after holding a towel to it for a few minutes. It still hurt like hell, though. "It would have been worse if not for those penalties against Arba."

"That doesn't matter to them," said Mark. "We're outsiders, Tyler. Twice over. Neither of us Drastovian, or from Krav. And we're referees."

Tyler rolled his eyes. "We're just enforcing the rules.

We're not monsters."

Mark laughed at him. "You really don't understand. I thought for sure that your goody-two-shoes routine was just that. But you truly don't get it."

"Get what?"

"Have you ever had a hard time in your life?" asked Mark.

"What kind of question is that?" asked Tyler. "I'm sitting in a locker room 6,000 miles from home, and you're asking me if I've ever had a hard time? You're looking at it."

Mark shook his head. "You *chose* this," said Mark. "You chose to come here, to try and make a go of it. You had that choice. You had agency. That's not a hard time, choosing between comfort and your dream. A hard time is not having a choice at all."

"I--"

Mark was on his feet now, pacing. "Those people out there, they haven't gotten choices their whole life. Half of them were raised under a dictator who gave them scraps to eat, and they thanked him for it. They didn't get to choose if they ate rotten potatoes for dinner. It was that or nothing. And sometimes it was nothing. Nothing for dinner, and nothing for breakfast the next day. The other half came of age just as they were blessed with democracy, and instead of a dictator giving them nothing, it was a government forgetting about them. They didn't even get rotten potatoes anymore. Their money taken from them and stuffed in the pockets of someone they've never met or even seen."

"I'm sorry for that, I truly am," said Tyler. "But I had nothing to do with that. I'm just trying to ref a football match."

"All those things that happened to them, all of them, were done by the rules. Never once did they get a say on those rules enforced upon them, but they were done by the rules nonetheless. They've been fucked over by the rules their whole life. That's what you are, mate. You're the rules, continuing to fuck them over. Their team is finally good again, and they have a chance to be something again, to rub it in the face of everyone who mocked them, and the rules are fucking them over again. So I'll ask you one more time. Have you ever had a hard time in your life?"

"I guess not," said Tyler.

"At least you can admit it," said Mark. "Keep that in your head. Always. They've had it harder than you. They will go further than you, when it comes down to it. You care about football. You traveled across the world to keep yourself a part of it."

"I love it," said Tyler.

"But you wouldn't kill for it," said Mark, not quite a question.

"Of course not," said Tyler.

"Then it's not everything to you," said Mark. He pointed at Tyler. "There's something inside you that knows it's just a game, a diversion. It is everything to them. It is life."

"Why do you stay here?" asked Tyler. "You're an outsider too. Why don't you go home?"

"I have my reasons," said Mark.

"You've said," said Tyler. "But there's no math I can do in my head that explains it. George said you're old friends with Vlad. He said you're in his pocket."

"You tell that old geezer to keep my name out of his mouth," said Mark. "It's none of his business, and it's none of yours as well. I'm making the best of a bad situation, and that's all you need to know. Understand?"

"Yes," said Tyler.

"Sometimes it's best not to know everything," said Mark. "And that goes double for you. You ready to go home?"

"Is it safe?"

"Of course fucking not," said Mark. "They'll be raging all day. But if we keep our heads down, we'll probably be left alone. Try not to get recognized."

"And if someone does recognize me?" asked Tyler.

"Then hit them over the fucking head," said Mark, and handed Tyler a blackjack.

"This will kill them," said Tyler.

"Yeah, quite possibly," said Mark. "Don't miss."

Mark unlocked the deadbolts and cautiously poked his head out. The hallways were clear and quiet. They hurried out of the arena, their bags slung on their backs, each of them palming a blackjack. As they got close to the street, the sounds of chaos could be heard. Glass breaking, fires burning, and shouting all echoed back to them. Tyler pulled his hood as low as he could, kept his head down, and they hustled down the road.

Their apartment was close, and most of the fans had spread throughout the town, sowing destruction or lapsing into drink farther away from the field. A few small groups moved past them without a second glance. A couple loners passed by, running toward whatever trouble they were looking for. No one was the wiser. They had forgotten them.

Tyler thought they were in the clear as they approached their apartment building. Once inside, they could breathe again and let the town settle down.

Three of them waited for Tyler and Mark. They wore bandannas over their faces, but they were all young men, none of which Tyler recognized. They spoke in Romanian. Mark answered them, and then one charged. Tyler's heart thumped in his chest, and he squeezed the blackjack tight in his palm.

Mark moved quicker than Tyler thought he could, flipping his blackjack out and hitting the first attacker solidly in the temple. He went down instantly, falling to the road like a stone. The second still charged, too late to change his mind. Mark caught him in his backswing on the chin, and he fell to the ground dazed. Mark booted him once, twice, three times in the ribs with hard, vicious kicks, and he stayed down. The third had hung back, and with glances at his two friends, he ran. Mark yelled after him in Romanian, and then spoke to the conscious one of the pair, grabbing him by the throat. After a few short sentences and harried nods by the downed attacker, they moved on, going into their apartment and locking the door behind them.

"Jesus," said Tyler, slumping down onto the couch. Mark retrieved two beers from their fridge and offered one to Tyler.

"To settle your nerves," said Mark. "You've never been in a fight?"

"Not like that," said Tyler. "How did you do that?"

"Do what?" asked Mark, taking a long swig of beer.

"Hurt them like that," said Tyler. "So casually."

"They intended to do us serious harm, my dear boy," said Mark. "And I took offense to it."

"What did you say to them?"

"I told them that next time I saw them, I wouldn't be so

merciful," said Mark.

"Christ," said Tyler.

"He has nothing to do with it," said Mark. "Aside from maybe putting the fear of God into 'em."

The sound of glass breaking from outside interrupted their conversation. Tyler parted the curtains to look, a pair of men smashing the front windows of the house across the street.

"How long will this last?" asked Tyler. "I need to check on Maria."

"Oh, I have no idea. Most likely by nightfall. I wouldn't worry about Maria. Vlad will take care of her. And even an enraged fan knows better to bother her anyway. Sit down, drink your beer, and relax."

Tyler went back to the couch, trying to do that. The beer helped a little, and he could feel the anxiety that tightened his body starting to loosen. He texted Maria. *Are you ok?*

He tried to forget his phone while he waited for her reply. It came quickly. *I'm ok. Are you?*

He replied. *Yes. Close call, but Mark took care of it.*

His phone buzzed again. *He's good at what he does. Stay inside, stay safe. Don't want you hurt.*

Tyler read her reply. He started typing a dozen times before settling on *Ok. Be safe. Talk to you soon.*

Mark flipped on the television, putting on an old sitcom from Netflix. One beer turned to two, to three, and he relaxed even as more glass broke outside, and he could see smoke rising from somewhere on the far edge of town.

Tyler did his best to follow Maria's advice, but his mind returned to her. She had such an effect on him, in such a short span of time. The day wore on, and the sun set. The discord disappeared with it, as order restored to Krav and the anger settled into a somber melancholy. People went home.

Some of them. As the sun disappeared, the roads emptied. The noise of chaos vanished. The town was quiet again, their dark apartment lit by the light from the television, filled with the sound of a studio audience. But then a familiar chant joined it outside.

It started as a distant atonal buzz at the edge of Tyler's hearing. He reflexively tried to swat away an insect from his ear before catching himself, realizing what he heard. He looked to Mark, who hadn't reacted.

The sound rose, getting louder and louder. The chants filled the town. *Krav Krav Krav.* They sang, the procession of red-robed townsfolk that Tyler couldn't see yet. They chanted a hymn he hadn't heard before. This was a dirge.

It was discordant, cacophonous. The hearing of it made him uneasy, and confused him. Why the different song? But then he realized. Krav had lost, and they sang a song of mourning. Mark still showed no sign of recognition.

"Don't you hear that?" asked Tyler.

"Of course I hear it," said Mark.

"And that's it? Nothing? No curiosity?" asked Tyler.

"It's none of my business, Tyler," said Mark. "And it's none of yours either. I'm going to sit here, and watch the telly, and drink until I fall asleep. I'd suggest you do the same. Anything you see out there will only end up hurting you."

The dirge got louder and louder in Tyler's ears as he sat and tried to ignore it. Soon it was all he could hear, and still it amplified, filling his mind, the atonal buzzing all that remained, and his vision filled with the split circle, it was all there was; it was everything, it was Krav, he couldn't do this anymore there was nothing but the split circle and he got up and went to the window and looked outside.

The street ran red. The procession filled it to overflowing, in every direction. They marched down Ofranda Road, hoods pulled up, obscuring their faces. They still raised the banners high, but they weren't the banners he recognized. All red banners had replaced the normal ones. No split circle, nothing but red, nothing.

Hundreds of them walked toward the pitch. Red hood after red hood passed, never looking up, only singing and chanting. The sea of red hypnotized Tyler. The song had him in its thrall. The river of crimson flowed down the road, and all he could do was watch. But then something broke its hold on him, and he closed his eyes, realizing he hadn't blinked in minutes, his eyes tearing up. The ocean of red wasn't perfect. There was one small incongruous drop in the surface. One not dressed in the red robe. A small stone carried along by the tide.

Tyler didn't understand from a distance. He couldn't make out what it was, the speck of white in the crowd. Who would they allow in their midst to break from tradition? The steward of the old ways? It made no sense.

But then they drew closer, propelled forward by the inexorable march. And Tyler then understood.

They passed underneath his window. The white stone in the river of red went by, and the stone was a man. One he recognized. It was Dario, the Krav player who missed the tying goal.

His face was blank at first glance, his eyes facing forward, marching with the crowd, still dressed in his white kit from the game earlier in the day. He didn't chant, though. As he drew closer, Tyler could see the fear in his eyes. Dario was trying to maintain a straight face, but the tears running down it betrayed him. He looked terrified.

And then he glanced up, looking directly at Tyler. Their eyes locked, and Tyler saw the fear amplified a thousandfold. Dario's eyes pleaded with him for help, for Tyler to rush outside, and help him, somehow, stop this red river from flowing. He cried for help, for anything Tyler could give. It was all in an instant, and Tyler could give him nothing. Dario looked ahead once again, their eye contact broken.

And then he was gone, carried away by the tide.

14

"They took him."

Mark's eyes fluttered open.

"Wha?" he asked, glancing at Tyler standing by the window, his head through the curtains.

"They fucking took him!" said Tyler. "Dario. The Krav player. The crowd has him!"

"Calm down," said Mark.

"You calm down," said Tyler. "They have him. God knows what they're going to do to him."

"What do you mean 'they have him'?" asked Mark.

"The procession," said Tyler. "They just passed outside. Smack dab in the middle of them was Dario. He looked terrified. Looked me right in the eyes. He was crying."

Mark stared at him. "And?"

"And what?" asked Tyler. "We have to do something."

"Why?"

"They're going to hurt him, Mark," said Tyler. "Punish him, for missing that shot. We can't let them."

"How do you know that?" asked Mark. Despite his drowsiness and his drinking, his voice was calm and rational. His eyes showed no worry or concern for Dario.

"Know what?" asked Tyler. "That they'll hurt him? Are you kidding me? He looked terrified. The town nearly killed itself earlier because they lost. You don't think they'd punish him for losing them the game?"

"Was he struggling? Fighting back against them?" asked Mark.

"No," said Tyler. "He was walking with them."

"So he was going willingly?" asked Mark.

"You didn't see his eyes," said Tyler.

"Okay," said Mark. "Let's say he was being taken by them, taken for some horrible punishment. What is your plan to stop them?"

Tyler stared at him.

"There are hundreds, if not thousands, of them out there," said Mark. "Whatever they have their mind set to, it will happen, and there's nothing two foreign blokes can do about it. Don't get involved. It's not our business."

"What are they doing?" asked Tyler. "You know more than you're telling me. It's the old ways. It's tradition. That's what everyone says. But none of that explains the look on Dario's face."

"I'm like a mushroom, Tyler," said Mark. "I get fed shit and kept in the dark, and in Krav, that suits me just fine. Whatever they intend for good ole Dario, it doesn't concern me."

"Just protect yourself, right?" asked Tyler. "Stand by and do nothing while someone is in danger?

"You're damned right," said Mark. "And I'm trying to protect you too, but you're too damned soft. Do your time and get out."

Tyler wanted to scream at him, but it wouldn't do any good. Mark was calloused to it. He had been here too long. There was no getting through to him. Tyler looked outside, his head craning through the curtains. The procession had moved past their apartment and turned toward the field. They were out of sight. The chants still echoed through the town, more distant now. He could go, sneak out, and catch up with the crowd. He could finally see what they were up to. But he was frozen. Was Mark right? Did he have any claim to interject himself in the traditions of an old town, one he had no stake in? Did he imagine the look of fear on Dario's eyes? It was a moment in time, a split second.

His phone buzzed and he looked at it. A text message from Maria. *Come over. Don't be seen.*

He responded. *Are you ok?*

She answered back. *I'm fine. I need to talk to you.*

He replied *OMW* and slid it back into his pocket. He pulled on his hoodie again. Mark's eyes were already closed again, dozing in front of the television. Tyler put on his shoes and was out the door.

The streets were quiet. He looked down the road that led to the field, seeing if he could see a single sign of the procession at ground level. He saw nothing. The faint echo of the chants rang back to him, but they lacked the same power they had earlier. He started toward Maria's small home, putting the red river behind him. Dario didn't need help. Maria did.

He walked briskly to her house, his footsteps all he could hear. The town sat vacant and dark, the few streetlights overhead serving as beacons in the darkness. He glanced into every window as he passed. All empty. Everyone in town was at Krav Field. They were all there, at the split circle.

Forget it, Tyler, worry about Maria.

They had taken Dario. He would pay for their loss. Someone had to suffer, someone had to take the burden of cost. It would be him. Tyler's mind felt heavy, suddenly, thoughts and voices filling it. He tried to keep walking but stumbled and fell to a knee. He held his head in his hands, trying to focus. And then a scream filled his thoughts, and another, and another. It was Dario. Screaming as they ripped him apart. They were paying the cost, paying it back in blood, he could feel the rents in Dario's flesh. Tyler could hear the chanting again, it filled his mind. They chanted for Krav, for her to accept the payment for their shame. He felt the blood, the warmth. Krav drank it in, taking it deep inside. They drained Dario dry, and the liters of blood redeemed the loss. The chants filled him, the assembled music floating in a morass of Dario's blood and gore.

Tyler felt Dario die.

And then he was freed, his head emptied of Dario's blood and chants for Krav. It was over. He opened his eyes, looking down at the cobblestone of Ofranda Road. How did he feel that? Why? Did they kill Dario?

Tyler felt the town beneath him now. Krav's pulse pounded, full of strength and vigor. Through the stones into the soles of his feet and into him, he sensed Krav, more than he could before. The same feeling as staring at the split circle, but closer. Krav crept inside him, insidious and strong, whetted with blood.

The chanting became stronger now, louder again. They were coming back. He realized that they would come this way. He needed to move and get to Maria's. It was safe with her. He hurried, every footfall connecting him with Krav.

He started jogging, and then running, but the chants, the dirge grew louder still. The low rumble shook his bones, and he felt Krav inside him. His feet slapped against the stones, and the red river ran behind him, the hundreds of Krav faithful on his heels, threatening to subsume him. He sprinted hard, his knees aching, sore from the day's game. He had to get to Maria's house, had to outrun the split circle.

Tyler could see her house and pushed himself. The chants were louder again, a volume he didn't think possible, the song so loud it would split the earth which would then swallow him whole. Krav would take him in her mouth, and he would slide down her gullet and be trapped inside for eternity. He would feed the monstrous town that had come alive, and the red river would flow over top of him.

And then he was at Maria's house, on her porch, the firm wooden boards underneath his feet, and he was alone. He looked back, and the street was still empty. No red robes in sight. The chants had vanished, not even a faint echo in his ears. Krav was quiet and empty.

I'm losing my mind.

Maria opened the door, repaired since this morning. It swung freely on the hinges.

"Your head," she said, pulling him in, looking at the wound on his scalp he had forgotten about. "Are you okay?"

"I'm fine," he said. He was worried about the inside of his head, not the outside.

"What happened?" she asked.

"Someone threw a bottle," he said.

"Savages," she said.

"I'll be alright," he said, gently pushing her away. "Are you okay?"

"No, I'm not okay," she said. She sat down on the couch, pulling him with her. "I thought I could trust him."

"Trust who?" asked Tyler.

"My father," she said. "I thought I could trust him. Above everything else, it was why I came here with him, why I stayed and tried to help fix Krav."

"What happened?" asked Tyler.

"After the game, during the riot, I went with him," she said. "To stay safe. And he was angry, angrier than I've seen in a long, long time. Since mother passed. He was destroying his office, knocking down trophies and plaques. I didn't try and stop him. I let him have his tantrum. And he seemed to calm down. We have a meeting after every game. To plan for the next game, about meetings for him the next few days. What's on the docket. You understand. But he didn't want to speak about any of that. He wanted to know if I thought I was pulling my weight. He asked me, point blank, if I was doing enough."

"I--"

"If *I* was doing enough," she said. She shook her head again. "The nerve of him. After his team loses the game, he dares to ask me if I do enough."

"What did you say?" asked Tyler.

"I said nothing," she said. "I would have only screamed at

him. I will not let my anger embarrass me. And he took this as an invitation to criticize me. To say that today's failure was my fault. To say that I didn't do enough to support him, to support Krav. It made me sick."

Tyler put his arm around her, holding her tight. "It'll be alright," he said.

"He forbid me from seeing you," she said. "Told me you were clouding my judgment. That you were taking my attention away from Krav. Forbid me. Me! I will not be told what to do, not by anyone, even him. How dare he! He wouldn't be coach, wouldn't be mayor if it weren't for me. His ideas, his suggestions, all come from me, are shaped by me. And he says that my judgment is clouded. He is the one who sees nothing but damned football, day or night. He loses sight of what is important." She took a deep breath. "Maybe there is no future for me in Krav."

"You should do what's best for you," said Tyler.

"I don't know what that is anymore," she said. "Father wants me at every game, from now on. He wants me under his thumb, in his pocket, like everyone else in Krav. I only stayed because we were equals. I will not stay to be controlled."

"I don't want you doing all this for me," said Tyler. She laughed, caressing his face.

"You're cute," she said. "And I do like you. But I do everything for me, first and foremost. No one controls me, not where I stay or go, and not who I enter into relationships with. And they do not question my focus, or my interests. I make those clear to anyone who needs to know. Maybe he doesn't need to know anymore."

"What should we do?" asked Tyler.

"Right now? Nothing," she said. "I will do what he says, for now. But I will keep my eyes and options open. And I will not stop seeing you. I enjoy you far too much." And she kissed him then, hard, sliding on top of him, straddling him. His hands were all over her, both of them pulling their clothes off, little by little, until they were both naked, having sex on the couch, and then on the floor. The golden aura returned, her touch setting off a fire inside of him.

All the thoughts of Krav, of Dario, of the red river didn't leave Tyler's mind, but his thoughts of Maria buried them. She subsumed them.

15

Tyler didn't sleep in the next day. He woke up early, before the sun rose, and couldn't fall back asleep. Maria had banished his vision of Dario's death out of his mind while she was awake. Now that she was asleep, it crept back in.

She slept peacefully, all the anger from last night gone, her beautiful face at ease. He could only lay in the low light and remember how he felt on the walk over. Remember feeling Dario's life leaving his body.

It made no sense. He saw Dario with them, and that's it. He couldn't have felt his death. He was imagining things. Had to be it. Krav was just a town. The split circle was just a symbol. He told himself over and over again, as the sun peeked over the horizon, the room slowly brightening.

He couldn't tell Maria. She wouldn't understand. She had

enough to worry about with her father. He had work with George today. George knew this town, knew it better than anyone. He could allay Tyler's suspicions.

Or confirm them.

He slipped out of bed in the dim light and got dressed. He kissed Maria goodbye and left, walking down Ofranda Road to George's shop. He could feel the Stone House leering at him from behind. It leaned down over him, leaning down over the whole of Krav. He didn't look.

It was all in his head. Krav was just a town. The split circle was just a symbol. The Stone House was just a house.

The streets weren't empty. Other laborers and workers beat their feet on Ofranda Road, heading toward work for the day. More than a fair few had bloodshot eyes from the night before. If that was the cost, they'd pay it gladly.

George wasn't in yet, and the front door was locked and gated. Tyler knew George left the back gate unlocked, so Tyler hopped the chain-link fence and went in that way, busying himself with organizational work and cleaning. There was always more to do, decades of accumulated filth that George never bothered with when he worked alone. Tyler let it consume him. It kept his mind off of Dario's screams as they flayed him alive.

A shout startled him as George entered, surprised to see Tyler there before him. The look of surprise left George's face and he comically grabbed his chest, breathing in and out. He walked over to Tyler, putting a permanently grease stained hand on Tyler's forehead, feeling it.

"What are you doing?" asked Tyler.

"Are you okay?" asked George. "You must be sick, coming in this early."

"You're very funny," said Tyler.

"I know," said George. "My mother always told me that. And she wouldn't lie to me. She was a good woman. Surprised to see you. How long have you been here?"

"An hour or so," said Tyler. "I couldn't sleep, so I came in. To take my mind off of things."

"If you'd like to take your mind off of things more often, feel free. The shop could use the cleaning," said George, putting down his things, surveying his tickets for the day. There were a handful of half-completed repairs that needed to be done. An old CRT television sat open, and George set to work. He was silent, not jumping into his typical rant or lecture to Tyler. Had he run out of material? That seemed impossible. George's well of complaints was bottomless.

"You're quiet today," said Tyler.

"Am I?" asked George. "Some days, my grievances cannot be summed up in words, Tyler."

"That bad, huh?" asked Tyler.

"It is no worse," said George. He paused, reflecting. "I am just running out of energy. It is a war of attrition, and I have only so much reserve." He thought again. "The dam will break eventually, without enough repair."

"That doesn't sound like you," said Tyler.

"Perhaps not," said George. "But more and more I wonder who I truly am. And what I am worth. What I add."

"Add to what?" asked Tyler.

"To life. To Krav," said George. "I ask more and more if Vlad was correct, to do what he did. He has the town on his side. Am I just being stubborn and bitter? Can I not handle a solution to a problem if I am not a part of it?"

"I don't think you're unreasonable," said Tyler. "If that

helps. You've lived here longer than most. You have a right to your opinion."

George's head stayed in the television, but he did not answer. Tyler needed to broach the subject of Dario. Now was as good a time as any.

"Have there been any disappearances since Vlad has taken over Krav?" asked Tyler. George stopped tinkering.

"Disappearances?" asked George. "Yes. Our nobility, our honor, our sense of self worth. All have disappeared."

"I'm serious," said Tyler.

"Why do you ask?" asked George.

"Last night," said Tyler. "I saw the procession again."

"Yes," said George.

"But it was different," said Tyler.

"It would have to be," said George. "They lost."

"Yes, the chants were different, the banners were different," said Tyler. "But it wasn't that. There was a man, walking with them. Without a robe or hood. It was a football player. His name was--is--Dario. He missed the tying shot in yesterday's game. He looked at me. He looked at me, up in my window, and he was terrified. I think--I think that the crowd did something to him."

"Why do you think that?" asked George.

Tyler paused. Should he tell George about his vision? The absolute terror and pain he felt in that moment, when the rivers of blood flowed from Dario's dying body? When he heard Dario's death rattle, the last bit of life leave him?

No, he couldn't. George would think he was insane. He needed to sound calm, and collected.

"It's just a feeling," said Tyler. "Have there been any disappearances since Vlad took over?"

George was quiet then, for over a minute, and he wasn't sure if George hadn't heard his question, or if he was ignoring it. Tyler was going to ask again, but George pulled his head from the television. His plain eyes stared at him.

"No, of course not," said George. His eyes betrayed nothing else, and he dipped into the TV. Another dead end. Tyler quietly sighed and started back to work. George's words interrupted him.

"I am reminded that we need a part from the hardware store. Can you run down and get it for me?" asked George.

"Sure," said Tyler. "Where is it?"

"It is called Surub. Turn left on Portocale Street, off of Ofranda. It will be on the right," said George. "Small store, but good people run it."

"What am I picking up?" asked Tyler.

"I will write it down," said George. "Their English is not so good." He scribbled on a scrap piece of paper and handed it to Tyler. It was in Romanian, and Tyler shoved it into a pocket. He started to go. George's words stopped him again, just as he was about leave.

"Funny you mention Dario," said George. "His parents own and run Surub. He worked there, for them." Tyler turned and met George's eyes. They were still unreadable, and George nodded slightly at him before turning back toward the television.

George knew something, but couldn't say it. He was leaving breadcrumbs for Tyler to follow. Tyler walked down Ofranda Road, turning left on a little street he had never noticed before, wide enough for a single car. Even then one wouldn't fit, because of the piles of crates and carts haphazardly stacked in front of one building or another.

Little shops lined the street, one selling produce, another selling fresh cooked chicken. The smell of the cooked meat followed him until he saw Surub. Compared to some of its neighbors, it was large. A sign spelled out the name of the shop with a symbol of a screw next to it. A telescoping gate stood pushed to one side, the entire store open to the street.

Tyler walked in. A small cat slept on a shelf. He pet it as he passed. Shelves lined every available space, narrow aisles made narrower. Cardboard boxes filled with nails and screws and nuts and bolts were stacked high on each shelf. Further inside he could see a back wall covered in shovels, rakes, and other tools. Fluorescent lights hung low over-head, and Tyler had to duck to not hit his head on a few. He saw a counter on the side of the store and navigated the maze of shelves and displays to make his way toward it.

He finally found it, an older man standing behind, stone faced, looking down. His thinning gray hair was cut short, and his hands held a notebook in front of him, scribbles of numbers and words in Romanian. He didn't meet Tyler's eyes as Tyler walked up.

"Hello," said Tyler. "George sent me for this." He handed over the piece of paper, hoping it was enough explanation. The man took it, glancing at it before passing it to the oth-er person behind the counter, a woman of similar age, her white hair tied up in a tight bun. She glanced at it and then at Tyler, and he saw her eyes for a split second before she walked off to get the needed part. They were red, bloodshot. She had been crying. Tyler looked back to the man's eyes, but saw nothing there.

Tyler waited awkwardly by the counter while the woman scrounged around somewhere in the store.

"George told me that Dario works here," said Tyler.

No, Tyler, he said he worked *here. George knows, just like you, that Dario died.*

"Said he's your son." The man's knuckles whitened as his grip tightened on the notebook in his hands. The cardboard bent.

"No," said the man. "No one else works here."

"Are you sure?" asked Tyler. "It doesn't seem like George would lie about something like that. Your son, Dario? Plays football?"

At mention of the word football, he squeezed harder, and Tyler could hear paper rip. His face was still blank, and now he turned his eyes up to meet Tyler's.

"No," said the man. "I have no son. We have no children." The woman returned, a paper bag full of whatever George had written down. She put it on the counter, and began to ring up Tyler on the register, hitting the big analog buttons on the old machine. She still refused to look Tyler in the eye.

"Are you sure?" asked Tyler. "You don't know anyone named Dario?"

"Yes," said the man, his voice short and hard. "Please, pay, and take your things."

He pulled out the cash that George had given him and handed it over to the woman, who opened the register and gave him his change. She met his eyes now, and the moment hung in the air as she handed over the change and the receipt. She had been crying. Sorrow filled them. She stared at him, and he recognized her eyes. They were Dario's eyes.

She pleaded for help with them, just like he had. She squeezed his hand as she gave him his change, squeezed it hard, as much strength as this woman had, and then she broke her gaze, looking back down and closing the register with a KA-CHING. Tyler smiled as pleasantly as he could at the man, even as the man's stone face stared him down.

Tyler took the small paper bag and left, petting the cat again on the way out. Another dead end. Would no one just talk to him and tell him what the hell was going on? Their own son, and they wouldn't say a word? They would deny him? What had Vlad done to these people? How could he have so much sway over them?

Tyler stopped in the street. What could he do now? Go back to George, and beg for more help? George, for all his talk of wanting to aid the town, was doing very little to help Tyler. Tyler wanted to scream. He still carried his change and receipt, and went to put them away in his pocket. But there was another piece of paper mixed in with it all. The woman had handed it to him.

It was the scrap paper George had given him, with the parts needed hastily scrawled on one side. But something else was written on the other side. By Dario's mother, when she was out of sight of her husband.

Four words, written in English, all capitals.

LOOK IN STONE HOUSE.

16

Tyler waited for the next away game before he went into the Stone House.

After returning from the hardware store that day, he didn't bring up the subject of Dario again to George, and George didn't hint at it, even once. George returned to his normal cantankerous self, complaining about tariffs on local farms and exports. They ate lunch together, like always.

If Vlad wanted to keep him and Maria apart, he did nothing to show it in the couple days before the next away game. He spent the nights there with her. He didn't ask her about Dario either, not yet. He needed proof. And that proof was in the Stone House.

Vlad took Maria with him. Maria went, playing along with Vlad's demand for now.

Krav was quiet. Every game was vital, any losses relegating Krav to Level 4 for another year. Everyone with the means traveled the few hours to the match. Mark drank on the couch when Tyler left for the night. Mark saw him leave, but said nothing. He had been drinking all day.

Tyler didn't follow Ofranda Road, the most direct route to the Stone House. The path the red river took. Instead, he headed toward the pitch. If there was anyone watching him, he'd make them work for it. In Krav, it seemed like there was always someone watching.

He walked toward the pitch, but instead of entering the stadium, he turned, circling around the outside edges, heading north. Scraggly scattered pine trees covered the sparse rocky land. A small flashlight lit his path. His feet contorted on the stony ground. He'd turn an ankle if he wasn't careful. One sprain and he couldn't ref. What would Vlad do then? Would the same unfortunate accident that befell his predecessor come for Tyler as well?

Before long he could see the House, peering at him from up on the hill in the distance. Its white stone reflected the small amount of moonlight, serving as a beacon. He could feel its windowed eyes staring at him. It judged him. It witnessed him.

He walked, avoiding the sharper rocks. The ground began to rise up beneath him, and would eventually meet with the slope of Ofranda Road, which curved its way up the hill that the great Stone House sat on. He would swing out, around the road, and come down on the house from above. If there was someone watching, they wouldn't be looking that direction. They'd expect visitors from town, not from the hilltop which no one lived on, too craggy and steep to be useful for much of anything.

Tyler climbed, his feet scrabbling for purchase on the rocky ground. Pebbles and stones scattered and slid behind him. They tumbled down the sheer surface. His feet slipped, and he had to go to his hands, trying to keep his balance as he climbed. His left hand came down on a jagged rock, and he felt a sudden flood of warmth from his palm. The edge of it had opened him up. His hand left splashes of red on the ground. He could suddenly feel his heartbeat, feel the flow of blood through him as it trickled out.

The rhythm of his heart thumped through his ears, reverberating through his body, into the ground. The ground echoed his heartbeat and then it was Krav's. He was back at the time of Dario's death, when he felt the earth swallow him whole and feel the life leave Dario's body. The blood, the blood. He had to cover it. He wore a plain black t-shirt, and he ripped the sleeve off, the fabric ripping unevenly. It was ugly, but it would work. He wrapped it around his cut hand, grabbing one end with his teeth and tying it. The tender flesh ached as the makeshift bandage put pressure on it, but he tightened it anyway. He couldn't feed Krav any more.

He paused. The blood beating in his ears slowed and then stopped. The sound of his own heart settled into the background again. He blinked, his vision normal again, and he set his eyes on the Stone House. It loomed over him, larger. It sat less than a mile away. How long had he been climbing? How much blood had seeped out of his hand into Krav?

He was close, almost to the level of Ofranda Road before it curved up and away from him, toward the Stone House. He continued to climb around the edge of the road. The scrub pines grew thicker now and he used them as handholds as he climbed higher. Every time his left hand closed on a branch or trunk he winced, but he did not let go, pulling himself along. There were less loose rocks here, the ground covered in dead pine needles. He couldn't see the Stone House directly. He could feel it, though. He knew it was there, staring down at the town. Being out of its vision felt good.

You're losing it, Tyler. The House is not alive.

He reasoned with himself as he climbed higher. He moved level with the House, and then past it. If he wanted to approach it from above, he could do it now, but he didn't stop. He would reach the top of the hill. He would see Krav, and the Stone House, from above.

Tyler's knees began to ache. The tender tendons that had once ruptured and exploded as he pivoted in the grass as a young man, then rebuilt and repaired, hurt as he put them under pressure. His breath came faster now, his heart beating harder, but nothing he couldn't handle. His cardio wasn't in question. It never had been. As a child he could run forever, and it was an advantage he always had playing football. The other kids would tire near the end of games, or practice. He never would. His breath never ended. His legs would betray him, his thighs or calves burning up, pushed too hard by his tireless lungs. It was fitting that his legs were the thing that finally gave up. They betrayed him after years of service, after years of being pushed too hard by a heart and lungs that would never stop.

His knees hurt, an ache that would linger into the night, even as he tried to sleep, a searing pain that burned like a cinder for hours. But he was near the top, and he pushed through. He found himself at the uneven top of the hill that bordered the northern edge of the town. He looked down on Krav and on the Stone House.

He saw how small it was from up here. He held the entire town within his vision. Tyler saw its limit, and it wasn't much. Inside it, it could feel claustrophobic. Harrowing, even. Here the cool wind whipped by him, pushing the thin needles of the sparse pine trees nearby. How far did the boundaries of Krav truly extend? Is it the southern bridge that marked the end of Krav? This hill? Was it anything the Stone House could see with its glass eyes?

He fixed his gaze on the Stone House. He couldn't stay up here all day, admiring the scenery. He had a mission. He started down the hill, slowly descending toward the Stone House. His gaze flitted back and forth from the ground in front of him, lit by his small flashlight and the House. He didn't know what it looked like from the northern side. Would there be more windows, looking to the hillside? With each step, more was visible, and there were no windows, only the mortared stone. It only had eyes for the town.

It also meant that Tyler couldn't see in. He saw a few doors at ground level as he got closer and Tyler used the trees as cover. But as far as he could tell, there was no one there at all. The House was shut up tight. If anyone was nearby, Tyler bet they waited inside. He left the shelter of the pine trees on the hill and scrambled down. Still no noise, no sign of getting spotted. He could see the front door, on the eastern and narrow part of the house, facing the end of Ofranda Road, which butted up against it. There was a wooden porch there, with a set of stairs. He walked around to the side, looking at his options in. There were two separate doors on the northern side, and a cellar on the western side, the twin doors locked with a padlock.

Both of the other doors were locked as well, but one was obviously newer than the other. The older door was thin and wooden. Tyler could hear the lock rattle when he tested it. He put his shoulder to it once, twice, and it gave way with a crack.

Tyler found himself in a utility room. He couldn't see anything in the dark. His flashlight revealed shelves filled with tools lining two of the walls and a door that led into the rest of the house. Tyler walked forward cautiously.

The boards of the wooden floor groaned with every step. The door led into a larger room, and immediately Tyler panicked. Red robes surrounded him. Walls of scarlet fabric pressed in.

They're just clothes, Tyler.

He stood in a wardrobe room, a big closet, with dozens of robes hung up on each wall, of all sizes. Tyler ran his fingers over the fabric, heavy and light and soft to the touch. He couldn't identify the material. An idea struck him, and he walked down the rows until he found one that matched his size. He threw it in his backpack, folding it down into the bottom.

He found the door out of the closet. He exited into a massive open space that took up the entire width of the first floor. A small riser stood to one side, with a podium ensconced at the front of it. This room smelled different than previous rooms. They had smelled of dirt and dust. A little like a locker room, a smell of human funk, covered up by a good amount of cleaning, but not erased entirely.

This room--this room smelled like metal. Or oil. Something deeper than dirt or sweat. The odor surrounded him, enveloped him. Tyler tried to breathe in through his mouth, but immediately felt nauseous. Letting it in at all was bad. He took shallow breaths. His flashlight swept over the floor, and he noticed a subtle change. The light revealed something painted in the middle of the flat space. He backed up and let his flashlight illuminate the entire thing, and then he saw it.

The split circle. Painted on the floor. It took up the entire space. He could feel a difference in the floor here. The boards felt different even than the others in the room. Tyler knelt down and grabbed at one, and it moved, moved as one with the entire split circle. It was a trapdoor of sorts. It didn't lead to the cellar though. That was somewhere else. This opened up onto the earth itself, and that same smell, that was strong before, hit him in the face. It was the smell of blood.

The ground here was the color of brick underneath his flashlight. The soil in Krav was light brown, like sand, except not here, not here because it was stained with the blood of a thousand sacrifices. It would bear that stain because it was older than him, older than the name Krav. It bore the mark of ancient blood rites that had sustained tribes of human before language had a name.

This had been in his vision, on Tyler's first day in Krav. A man had been sacrificed here, on the dirt floor, surrounded by people, and white stone.

He coughed and closed the lid of the trapdoor, closing the split circle, and he could see the painted symbol on top of the wooden floor was blood, dark and red. But it was dry to the touch.

It's dry because they don't sacrifice them here anymore.

This was vestigial, a remnant. The vision was something that happened long ago.

But who was the woman, from the other vision? The question remained.

They had taken Dario to the pitch.

Dario. Tyler remembered his mission here. He needed evidence of Dario's disappearance. Dario's mother had sent Tyler here, known there was another bread crumb. Tyler moved on, leaving the smell of copper and heavy metals behind him.

What would there be? He left the large room, looking for stairs. He went the way he hadn't gone yet, toward the front door. He found a stairway, recessed and off to the side. Still no sign of anyone else here. Did they really leave no guard? Maybe they assumed no one would try to break in.

He sneaked upstairs, the wooden staircase creaking beneath him. How old was this house? How many times had they replaced these stairs? He stood on the second floor now, and in front of him was a long hallway, with many doors on each side. They opened into a small room with a bed and a small nightstand. The southern rooms all had a window in each. The house's eyes. A candle sat behind each window, on an inside sill. The beds were all bare mattresses. Someone had once stayed here, but now there was nothing. The entire second floor was just empty bedrooms. Nothing.

No, not empty. He opened the drawer on a nightstand, and there was a book inside. Worn, written in a foreign language. It fell apart in his hands.

He went to the next room, and there was another, in the same place. This one in better shape. This one was newer, but still the same contents. He stuffed it into his backpack.

Another mystery.

He went upstairs to the third floor. Another long corridor, with doors lining each side. The same windows, with candles on every sill. The rooms were all empty here. No beds, no furniture at all. What was this place? Tyler returned downstairs, still no sounds other than his own footsteps. Where else was there to search?

The cellar.

But where were the stairs down? He returned to the first floor, walking back through the large room. He avoided the split circle. There was a small door he missed in the far corner. That had to be it.

He went through the door, and there were a set of downward stairs. Tyler pointed his light down into the darkness of the cellar. He walked down.

The cellar wasn't huge, the walls the same mortared stone as the rest of the house. The floor was the packed dirt of the hillside. Boxes sat everywhere, stacked up to the roof. He grabbed the nearest one and pulled it open. His light revealed red. Red robes rolled into tight bundles filled every box. He closed it, wandering through the tight maze the boxes created. There had to be something else. Had to be. But there were only boxes. It was just damned storage. He swept his flashlight through the room, looking for anything out of place. There was nothing.

Wait. His flashlight danced over something, something slightly different.

There was a different-sized box. No, not even a box, but a trunk. A heavy trunk, made of wood and iron, tucked far back in a corner.

He ran to it and undid the locking metal clasp. He pulled

the lid open, shining his flashlight inside. The contents reflected at him. Jewelry filled the chest. Rings, necklaces, earrings, bracelets. Thousands of pieces, stacked deep and dense. His mind reeled in confusion.

Jewelry?

And then he realized that this was what was left of the victims. All that he would find of Dario would be right here.

Think, Tyler, think.

He tried to picture Dario in his mind, running across the field. What jewelry did he wear? Was it a ring? No, no rings. Earrings, a simple bracelet?

He pictured him on that day, Grigore passing the ball to him and Dario kicking and missing. His whole body slumping when he saw he had missed.

Tyler saw it in his mind's eye. A gold chain floating gently around Dario's neck as he crossed the field. A chain, with a thin silver circlet at the end.

Tyler's eyes searched inside. It would be on top. Still, there were thousands of pieces inside, some quite old, the metal starting to pit and stain. He saw Dario's necklace, and he grabbed it, stuffing it into a pocket. He took a picture with his phone for good measure of the contents of the trunk.

Voices interrupted him from outside. They filtered down into the cellar. Two men spoke in Romanian.

Shit.

Then the sound of them unlocking the padlock on the door. They were coming down.

Tyler closed the trunk, locking the metal clasp, leaving everything as it was. There was a small space in the opposed corner blocked off by boxes. He sneaked into it and crouched, turning off his flashlight. They wouldn't be able to see him unless they searched thoroughly.

He heard the padlock unlock and then slide off the door. It opened, and then their flashlights lit up the cellar. They were speaking in Romanian, two loud, brusque voices. He heard them step down.

Tyler's heart thudded in his chest. He tried to control his breathing and stay quiet. They would kill him if they found him, they'd bleed him just like they'd bled Dario, like the thousands of others over the years, his belongings ending up in a forgotten trunk in a basement--

One light swept right in front of him, over to the trunk. They walked over to it, both of them, still talking, arguing. He saw only their silhouettes, and he couldn't recognize them. If they turned around, they would see him crouched there. One reached down and opened the trunk, doing the same thing Tyler just did, surveying the contents. He scooped a handful of the jewelry, stuffing it into a pocket. The other said something else, but then did the same, each taking a share of loot.

Don't look at me don't look at me don't look at me--

The trunk shut, and their lights spun around, but neither shone on Tyler. They walked upstairs, closing the basement door behind them. They had left the outer double door open. Tyler forced himself up, as quiet as he could, and crept up and outside the house. The night hid him. He looked for others. Seeing no one, he ran, back up into the relative cover of the pine trees on the hillside.

17

Tyler waited for Maria in her house when she came back from the away game early in the morning. He sat on the couch in her small living room.

She was surprised to see him, but not unhappy.

"Tyler!" she said. "I thought you'd be at your apartment."

"We need to talk," said Tyler.

"Can it wait?" she asked. "I've been on a bus for six hours today."

"No, it's waited long enough," he said. He tossed Dario's necklace onto the coffee table in front of him, followed by the book he had grabbed in the house.

"What are those?" asked Maria.

"It's a necklace, and a book," said Tyler.

"I can see that, Tyler--"

"It's Dario's necklace," said Tyler. "I'm sure you know him. Or knew him. Wasn't on the bus today, was he?"

"No," said Maria, picking up the jewelry, examining it, rolling it between her fingers. "Father said Dario left town."

"Is that what he said?" asked Tyler. "Strange, then, that he managed to put his necklace in a trunk in the basement of the Stone House before he left. Seems odd to me."

"What?" asked Maria.

"I went into the Stone House," said Tyler. "In the cellar, there is a wooden trunk, filled with jewelry. Dario's necklace was right on top. His mother told me to look for him there."

"You shouldn't have done that--"

"No," said Tyler, cutting her off. "I'm done following the rules around here. You know what's going on, and all I get is the runaround. I want answers, Maria. No more avoiding it. What is going on in Krav? What happened to Dario? They took him to the pitch the other night, and he never. Came. Back." He grabbed the necklace from her. "This is all that is left of him!"

"No," said Maria. She was shaking her head. "No, father said that was over. He told me we were changing things. Bringing Krav back into the light--"

"What are you talking about?" asked Tyler. He got up, grabbed her by the shoulders. Maria's eyes darted back and forth. "Maria, look at me." Her eyes met his. "Your father said *what* was over?"

"The sacrifices," she said. "The blood.'"

He pulled her over to the couch and they sat down.

"Please," said Tyler. "Tell me what is happening in Krav. What did they do to Dario?"

"He promised me. Father promised me he wouldn't let

it come to this," said Maria. "Another thing he lied about. Another broken promise."

"Slow down," said Tyler. "Start with the sacrifices."

"I can't tell you," said Maria. "It's too dangerous. They'll kill you for knowing. You're an outsider. You're not supposed to know the old ways."

"I don't care," said Tyler. "Tell me."

She sighed, and stared at him. "This is what my father told me. Before Krav had a name, there were the old ways. The people here, they valued the land, above all else. They had been there since it was young, and they cherished it. They took care of it. They defended it against invaders. They farmed on it, they raised their children on it. They took care of it, and it took care of them. For generations, this was how it went. At a certain point, that care, that *love*, it turned to worship."

"And that worship turned to sacrifice," said Tyler.

"It was easy, back then," said Maria. "There was more room for belief, for faith. And when someone attacked the land, the people gave the land their blood. When someone betrayed the land, the betrayer paid for it. When someone failed the land, they repaid their failure. Before there was Drastovia, there was Krav. And the old ways did not change just because Krav now had a name. No matter who ruled the country, or what happened outside of Krav, the old ways remained. And Krav remained. And that convinced all the people that their worship and their sacrifice was worthwhile. Because Krav persisted, despite war and plague, despite everything."

"How many people have died here?" asked Tyler.

"Over centuries? Thousands," said Maria.

"But it was ancient history by the time your father was born, right?" asked Tyler.

"It was history," said Maria. "But not ancient. My father's parents saw people bled to death, and they still told stories of the old ways to him as a child. But Stroescu strangled it out, just like he strangled Krav. And some tried to keep it alive, but they failed, and Krav slowly suffocated, and my father left."

"And when you came back," said Tyler. "He brought back the old ways. And connected them to football."

"Yes," said Maria. "And he lied to me. Lied to my face! He told me all of this. Told me the history of Krav. Showed me the hole in the Stone House where the ground is forever red. Told me that by bringing the old ways back, he would connect the town again, bring it back to life, but avoid the bloodshed. He showed me the vista, told me that story, and asked for my help. And I promised it. I promised to help him as long as he was peaceful. And I helped him. And now Dario is dead."

"You didn't know," said Tyler.

"There's no excuse," said Maria. "Blood is on my hands."

"What's in this book?" asked Tyler. "There was one in every room. I can't read it."

"I recognize it," she said. "But I can't read it. It's not in Romanian. Father always said it was old folk tales. Stories about Krav. Ask George. He might know."

"What can we do?" asked Tyler.

"I don't know," said Maria. "The police are a part of it. The whole town is a part of it. Did anyone see you there?"

"No," said Tyler. "A couple of locals came in, but I sneaked past them. They didn't know I was there."

"At least we have the element of surprise," she said. "Do we really know Dario is dead? There's no body."

Tyler hesitated. "I felt him die," he said, finally.

Maria looked at him, confused. "What?"

"I felt him die," said Tyler. "The other night. I didn't tell you. I didn't know what to tell you. It makes no sense, but it happened."

"What happened?" asked Maria. "You're not making any sense."

"Krav lost. Mark and I escaped and holed up in our apartment. I saw the procession come through town, and I saw Dario. Right in the middle of them. But he wasn't wearing a red robe or hood. He was still dressed in his kit. And he looked up and saw me."

"What did he do?" asked Maria.

"Nothing," said Tyler. "He looked up at me, and I saw a desperation in his eyes, in just a split second. But then he looked away, and he continued walking with them. Then you texted me, and I came here. And on the way, I felt him die."

"How?" asked Maria.

"I don't know," said Tyler. "It felt like I was dying. I could feel his fear. He was so afraid, Maria. He wanted his mother. He was afraid, and then they killed him. They cut him to the bone and bled him into the ground. And I felt every moment. I felt his last breath. I felt him die, and then there was nothing."

Maria wasn't looking at him now, her eyes down. She looked at him, her face unreadable.

"You couldn't feel him die, Tyler," she said. "That's impossible. You must have imagined it."

"It didn't feel imagined," said Tyler. "It felt real. I felt them cutting him open. I think--" He stopped there, stopped himself from finishing the sentence. He was going to say that Krav made him feel that. That the town itself had connected itself to him and delivered Dario's death rattle to him. And the visions, the visions of sacrifice, of the poor woman, dying in her bed.

But if him feeling Dario's death was insane, what was the idea of Krav being alive? He couldn't engage with the thought, certainly couldn't say it out loud. It would make it truth, and Tyler couldn't let that thought take root in his mind. Krav wasn't alive. Krav *wasn't* alive.

"You think what?" she asked.

"I think Krav isn't safe anymore, if it ever was," said Tyler. "And we should think about leaving."

"We can't just leave," said Maria.

"They're killing people," said Tyler. "And that's just after a loss. What happens if Krav doesn't get promoted? A massacre?"

"That hasn't happened yet," said Maria.

"It doesn't matter," said Tyler. "That's how these things go. The people want blood. They want the old ways."

"They just want their pride back," said Maria.

"What does it matter what they want?" asked Tyler. "People are dying."

"It's my father, Tyler," said Maria. "Maybe he doesn't know. Maybe I can get him to stop it."

"Don't try and sell me that," said Tyler. "Your father knows everything that happens in this town. Everything. Now he is suddenly unaware when thousands of people sacrifice a man in the middle of the football field?"

"I have to be sure," said Maria. "I can't go on necklaces and feelings. I need to *know* before I abandon my father. What about your career? What about football?"

"I don't want to leave it behind," said Tyler. "But it's not worth anyone's life."

"You can leave, Tyler," said Maria, looking into his eyes. "My father won't hurt me. You can go. Be safe." She touched his hand, her skin warm. It was ambrosia, and his mind buzzed.

"I can't leave you here alone," said Tyler. "I won't. We just have to be careful."

"If Krav keeps winning," said Maria. "Maybe there won't be any more sacrifices."

Tyler didn't answer that, only brought Maria close to him, putting his arm around her, her head on his chest. She looked up at him, with her big, beautiful eyes, and he felt a twinge of something, a familiar, unearthly feeling, but then it was gone. She kissed him, and it felt good. It felt right.

He had meant what he said to her, that he couldn't leave her here alone.

As they kissed, and then made love, he knew it to be true, as sure as anything. He wouldn't leave Krav without Maria.

18

Tyler and George sat outside, in the small backyard of George's shop. The sun shone down on Krav, and on them. George had brought dumplings, and there was no getting over how good they were. But Tyler's mind wasn't on the food, not today.

"Tell me you weren't involved with that man's death," said Tyler, finally. He had barely spoken all morning. Sleep had been hard to come by the night before. Every time he closed his eyes, he felt Dario dying again. He felt the last shudder of breath as he died. Tyler saw the red robes and the shadowed faces. Maria slept peacefully.

Walking through town the next morning, on the way to George's shop, was no better. He eyed everyone he passed. Were they there? Were they complicit? Had they worn the red robe? Had they held the knife that ended Dario's life?

He could feel their eyes on him as he walked down Of-randa Road. *They knew they knew they knew they knew*

If George had noticed his silence, he hadn't acted any differently, spouting off about the potholes, about the road conditions, about the lack of infrastructure improvements after decades of decay.

George said nothing after Tyler spoke, not for a long while. He ate a dumpling slowly, which was his way, slathering it in sour cream before taking small bites. He didn't look at Tyler once during this. Tyler stared at him. Waiting. Finally, after chewing and swallowing the last of his dumpling, George looked at him, meeting his stare.

"You really believe I had a hand in that?" asked George. His hard eyes stared at Tyler.

"I don't know what to believe anymore," said Tyler. "I need to hear it from you. I need to know I can trust you."

"You should trust no one," said George. "You are alone here. A stranger in a strange land. I had nothing to do with his death. I was making dumplings at home, like many nights." Tyler saw nothing but the truth in his eyes, and he looked away.

"They killed him, George," said Tyler. "They bled him in the middle of the field. They fed the split circle."

George shook his head, eating another dumpling. "I cannot speak on that."

"No more of that," said Tyler. "You need to talk. You need to tell me. I have to know what I'm facing. Maria told me what she knows, but there are still holes."

George's face changed at that, softening slightly. "What did she tell you?"

"You talk about the old ways, and she says that they killed people back then too. I found the jewelry, decades, hell, centuries old jewelry in a trunk in the Stone House--"

"You went in the house?" asked George. "You should not have done that, it is not safe--"

"No one saw me," said Tyler.

"It doesn't matter," said George. "They will know. Vlad will know."

"How will he know?" asked Tyler. George shook his head already, preemptively. "George, tell me."

George stopped eating. He left an unfinished dumpling on the small napkin placed in front of him. The sour cream slowly slid off of it, warming in the sun.

"Krav will tell him," said George, finally, a great breath leaving him afterward, as if it pained him to say it. "Krav will tell him everything."

"What the hell does that mean?" asked Tyler.

"She talks to him, I imagine," said George. "And she sees everything that happens here. There are no secrets from her. She saw what you did. And if she wants Vlad to know, he will know."

"How do you know that?" asked Tyler. George stared at him again, not wanting to answer. He relented. Tyler was watching long held defenses fall, moment by moment.

"Because she used to speak to me," said George. "When I needed answers, or advice, or comfort, she was there."

"Krav was there?" asked Tyler. He thought back to his vision of Dario's death. "The town? Did you just hear a voice?"

"No," said George. "No voice. She would show me things. Things happening around town. Unrest, sometimes conflicts between people. And I would help them. Or try.

Sometimes I failed, but you cannot succeed if you do not try. And the people deserved someone trying to help."

"Visions?" asked Tyler.

"I suppose," said George. "But that word is too small. I did not just see things. I felt everything. I was *inside* her."

The feeling of Dario's last breath rose to the surface. The visions of sacrifice.

"You cannot understand. Even those in Krav sometimes struggle with it. But she is real, and she feels us all."

"I believe you," said Tyler.

"You do?" asked George.

"Krav showed me Dario die," said Tyler. George's face turned to confusion. "And other things. Things that don't make sense."

"Krav spoke? To you?" he asked. "That cannot be. She will only speak to the steward, and whoever it is, it is not you."

"I felt Dario die, George. I was there. I felt it coming through me, up through Ofranda Road. If that wasn't Krav talking to me, what was it?"

George questioned him with his eyes. "If that is true, if Krav is speaking to you, while Vlad leads..." He trailed off, his eyes glazing over. His mind engaged in alien calculus.

"George," said Tyler. "George!"

George blinked, his eyes refocusing.

"I don't care if you believe me or not," said Tyler. "I saw what I saw. What does this say?" Tyler pulled the book out from his bag, and handed it to George.

"You've been busy," said George. "You should not have taken this."

"I know, I know," said Tyler. "What does it say? Maria

said it's not in Romanian."

"It is in the old language," said George. "The language of Krav. She was not born here. She would not know it."

"What is it about? There were a lot of them, up in the house."

"They are stories of Krav," said George. "Folk tales. Legends. Myths."

"About what?" asked Tyler.

"What are any old stories about? About creation. Hubris. They serve to teach us with simple stories with big characters."

"Nothing else?" asked Tyler.

"To me? No," said George.

"What about someone else?"

"Some consider them more than stories," said George. "Some think they tell the future."

"Prophecy?" asked Tyler.

"Perhaps," said George. "Why do think Vlad is so sure that Krav will succeed?"

"What do they say?"

George stared at him. "They say a righteous man's sacrifice will drag Krav back into the sun. That he will love Krav, and make her a god."

"Does Vlad think that's him? What would his sacrifice be?"

"Most likely coming back home," said George.

"He think it's fate?"

"Yes," said George. "But that is foolishness. He is no hero, even if Vlad would like to paint himself as one."

How many people has he killed?"

George shook his head. "I do not know. Too many. Any

is too many. I do not know the true number, but even a blind man would notice the disappearances. And Dario is the most flagrant yet. He feels untouchable, Vlad does. And so be makes more and more of a statement of his power. Dario loses the football game, and so he pays the price. And then Krav FC plays better the next game. It keeps Vlad in control, in power."

"But why doesn't Krav, the town, why doesn't she do something about it?" asked Tyler. "You said she comforted you. Used you to help people, right?"

"She is powerful," said George. "But she exists to serve us. And she changes to suit our wants and needs. You saw the pounds of gold and silver up in the house. For a long time, they fed Krav with blood, and she grew, and so they fed her more. Did they need to sacrifice hundreds and hundreds of people over the years? Feed her young and old alike? Did she need the blood for the crops to grow, for the people to flourish? No, she didn't."

"You stopped the sacrifices," said Tyler.

"While I was steward, Krav was not given anyone," said George.

"Maria told me Vlad was told stories about it as a child," said Tyler. "But that no one was killed since he was born."

"Not true," said George. "But expecting the truth from Vlad is an expectation I gave up long ago. I saw a neighbor die when I was a child. We were suffering under Stroescu. Had been, for a long time. So they killed her. It did not ease our suffering. It only created more death."

"When did it stop?" asked Tyler.

"When I stopped it," said George. "After Vlad left, in search of his destiny. I stayed, and I became the steward of the old ways, and I put an end to the death, to the blood. It was hard fought. There were still many who wanted to continue. It was what we always did. But I stopped it. I turned the house on the hill into a meeting hall and dormitory for those put out by Stroescu policies. I did this. And Krav survived, and Stroescu was eventually overthrown, and we got democracy. But that was not enough."

"Maria told me Vlad promised no deaths," said Tyler. "No sacrifices."

"He made no promises to me," said George. "But he remains a liar. I knew from the moment he returned, with the promise of making Krav better, that he had ill intent. He does not care about Krav. He cares about himself."

"What can we do?" asked Tyler.

"Are you volunteering, Mr. Hero?" asked George.

"I just want to help," said Tyler. "What will it take to stop it?"

"A miracle," said George. "Krav herself is on his side. What can we do in the face of that?"

Tyler remembered the vision. The feeling he had as he climbed up the hill, bleeding into the earth. Does she feel it all? Does she see it all? George looked defeated, and the dumplings were gone. The shop was quiet for the rest of the day. Tyler was happy to leave.

Mark wasn't alone in the apartment when he came home. Raul and Iosef were there with him. The table was filled with empty bottles.

"We've been waiting all day, mate," said Mark.

"I was working," said Tyler. "What do they want?"

"What do you think?" asked Mark. "A meeting with Vlad."

"Tell them he can fuck off," said Tyler.

"I'm not telling them that," said Mark. "I like having my head still connected to my body."

"I'm not talking to that killer," said Tyler. "I don't speak Romanian, but I bet they recognize the name Dario." Both Raul and Iosef's eyes flicked to Tyler. "He was your teammate, and he's dead. Do you not care? Anything for Krav? Even watching your friends murdered, and doing nothing?"

Both of them looked away.

"I see you both have the decency to feel shame," said Tyler.

Raul said something in Romanian to Mark, and Mark nodded.

"Tyler--"

"Don't Tyler me," he said. "Am I supposed to go walk into the lion's den with a smile on my face?"

"No, but you are supposed to value your own life," said Mark. "If you keep yelling at these men, they will beat you, and then carry you to Vlad. It's not worth the pain. Let's go."

Mark's face was not one of scorn or anger, only weariness. "Please, just go peacefully," said Mark, his voice pleading.

Tyler stared at him, and then nodded, relenting.

"Fine," said Tyler. "Let's go." They walked, with Raul in front, Iosef in back, toward the field and its offices. A storm front had moved in and it began to drizzle on them as they approached. It poured by the time they got to the stadium. Vlad waited for them in his office.

Mark walked inside, and Tyler went to follow him, but was stopped by Raul and Iosef. They motioned for him to wait outside. The door to the office closed, and Tyler waited, standing against the wall, like he was in college again, waiting for a classroom to let out. Raul and Iosef wouldn't meet his eyes, and the hallway was otherwise empty. The walls and door to Vlad's office were thick, but he could still hear the tone of their conversation. Muffled deep tones, and the minutes crawled by.

Then there was shouting, both voices barking back and forth at one another. Neither Raul or Iosef betrayed any concern on their face, and the yelling got louder and louder until finally, it stopped. The voices continued, almost inaudible again, and then Mark opened the door. He looked defeated, any ounce of fight left in him erased. Their eyes met, and Tyler read them. The look was one of pity.

And then he was gone, leaving Tyler alone.

"Tyler," said Vlad, from his chair.

Tyler paused, and then entered. Vlad was smiling, but his red face betrayed the shouting match he had with Mark.

"Trouble in paradise?" asked Tyler.

"Oh, no," said Vlad. "Mark just needed to be reminded about his priorities."

"What would those be?" asked Tyler.

"His health, of course," said Vlad. "And his career. Both very important things."

"Seems Krav is awfully dangerous to people's health lately," said Tyler.

"Why do you say that?" asked Vlad.

"I think you've recently lost a player," said Tyler. "Dario."

"Dario couldn't deal with the shame of losing the match," said Vlad. "And so he fled. The people here are exacting about their expectations."

"Fled?" asked Tyler. "Is that the story you're going with?

His mother's tears told me a different story."

"I'm sure she's upset about her son's failure," said Vlad, his face joyless. "Failure has a cost."

Tyler stared into Vlad's dead eyes. Vlad wouldn't incriminate himself, or talk of Dario's death.

"What do you want, Vlad?" asked Tyler.

"I needed to speak to you two before tomorrow's game," said Vlad. "I thought it was time for a change."

"Are you firing us?" asked Tyler. "I thought you needed us."

"Oh, we do," said Vlad. "You and Mark both. A good change. At least for you. You've done well so far in Krav, Tyler. You should be rewarded. I am promoting you to head referee. Mark will work under you from now on."

"What?" asked Tyler. "Why now? Do you expect me to suddenly play ball now that I'm head ref?"

"I expect you to do what is right for you," said Vlad. "It is in your best interests to help Krav. To help Maria. To help yourself. You can have whatever you want, Tyler. Remember that."

"I'm not in the business of helping killers," said Tyler.

Vlad smiled then, or his attempt at one.

"I am no killer," said Vlad. "I am only a servant of Krav. I do what she requires. Sometimes I have my doubts, Tyler, as I'm sure you do. About what is right, and what is wrong. But at the end of the day, Krav smiles upon me, and then I know. Just as you will know. You will understand. But do not forget. Failure has its cost."

19

It was game day again. Tyler and Mark sat in the locker room. Mark hadn't said two words to him since the meeting late yesterday. It was an hour until game time.

The deadbolt on the door was locked. Mark's voice startled him.

"He saved me, you know," said Mark.

"What? Who saved you?" asked Tyler.

"Vlad," said Mark. "Vlad saved my life."

"How?" asked Tyler.

"It was in London," said Mark. "We played on the same team, him and I. This was before he hurt himself. Man, could he play. Quick, strong for his size, but most of all, smart. His football IQ was off the charts. He knew where everyone else on the field would be before they did. You'd be running with him, and he'd put the ball right where it and you needed to be. Made me look a lot better than I was. I was on my way out, anyway. I couldn't hang with 'em."

"You played with Vlad?" asked Tyler.

"Yeah," said Mark. "Only for a bit. But we became fast friends. We both breathed the sport. And he proved how much of a friend he was when I dropped out. I didn't want to leave London. My whole life was there. He suggested being an official. He knew someone, in the league office, and they got me a gig. Kept me in London, kept me in football. He was a true friend."

"And that saved your life?" asked Tyler.

"No no no," said Mark. "I mean, it helped me, but I would have survived. Would have played for some small team in some pissant town, and I would have been fine enough. That was the start, to give you an idea. The saving was later. I grew up poor, Tyler."

"Sorry," said Tyler.

"Don't want your sympathy," said Mark. "Just the facts as they are. I grew up poor. Didn't really think about it at the time, but it changes how you think. Life was always about survival when I was young. Making sure I got food every day. My dad, God rest his soul, doing whatever he could to give us a roof over our heads. We were taught to do what was necessary to survive. And you don't lose it. It's ingrained in you. It's inside you. And so you keep scrabbling for more when you don't really need it. And you go to dangerous lengths to do it."

"What happened?" asked Tyler.

"I fell in with some bad people," said Mark. "Some I knew from when I was younger, others as drinking buddies. I don't remember how I met some of them, honestly. Probably to do with the drinking. But soon I was gambling. Gambling a lot. And sometimes, I won. Happy days. But mostly, I lost. And then I started owing money. To the kind of people who were my friends, until I owed them money, and then they weren't so friendly. Vlad tried to warn me. He tried, but I didn't listen. Then some men came to collect. I didn't have it. If I had it, I would have paid."

"What happened?" asked Tyler.

"I killed them," said Mark. "They threatened me. They didn't have guns. Probably figured they didn't need them against me. I beat them to the death with a cast iron frying pan."

"Christ," said Tyler.

"I was running on adrenaline, but killing them was only postponing the inevitable. My friends would send more men after me. Vlad saved me. Got me out of London, out of the country."

"Brought you here," said Tyler. "To Krav."

"Yes," said Mark. "Far away from my friends who wanted me dead. Someplace no one would look. Krav. Gave me work, protected me."

"Is that why you were shouting with Vlad yesterday?" asked Tyler.

"No," said Mark. "I mean, it matters, but it wasn't about us. It was about you."

"Me?" asked Tyler.

"Yes," said Mark. "He means to throw you to the wolves, I think. Give you just enough rope to hang yourself with. It's what he always does. Puts you into a position where you have to do what he wants. He knows your relationship with

Maria. He knows you know about Dario. By making you head official, he's making you complicit. You're in charge now."

"Does he expect me to call the games for Krav?" asked Tyler.

"I think he expects you to do what everyone does," said Mark. "And that's work with him."

"He's a killer," said Tyler.

"So am I," said Mark. "Doesn't mean as much as you think it does."

"You were defending yourself," said Tyler. "They would have killed you."

"You don't think he can't justify Dario's death?" asked Mark. "He didn't kill him. Someone else's hands did. He might not have even been able to stop them."

"He let it happen," said Tyler.

"It doesn't matter, right now, today," said Mark. "What are you going to do?"

"In today's game?"

"Yeah."

"I'm going to call it like I always call it," said Tyler. "Straight down the middle. What are you going to do?"

"You're in charge," said Mark. "Vlad told me that himself. I follow your lead. Call what you tell me to."

"Straight down the middle," said Tyler.

"Down the middle it is," said Mark, smiling.

The arena had started to rumble then, the Krav faithful filling the stands, shaking the place like thunder. They danced and chanted for Krav.

As game time approached, Tyler and Mark went out on the field, doing their normal warm-ups. Both teams were out there, and the atmosphere was electric. Only three games remained, and Krav needed to win all of them to advance. They played against Vuhl today, their kits dark purple. Mark had said they were good for Level 4, but the same size difference was clear between Krav FC and them. Tyler saw no purple in the stands. Vuhl fans apparently didn't travel very well. Or maybe they had heard about what had happened at the last home game and opted out. Either way, the Krav faithful occupied every seat. The singing had already begun. Grigore was amping up the crowd as usual, jumping up and down, his massive legs propelling him high into the air. His arms windmilled above his head.

He didn't look in Tyler's direction, but Vlad did. Vlad smiled his indeterminate smile and nodded at Tyler. Tyler didn't know what it meant, but it wouldn't change his behavior. He would honor the game.

Soon, it was time. Tyler's heart beat hard in his chest, and the chants rose around him, higher and louder, until they surrounded him and filled the pitch. The field responded to the noise. It bombarded him with emerald. He was in charge now, and he couldn't let the explosions of sound and color overwhelm him. He had to call the match.

The game began, and Krav jumped out quickly, Grigore charging down the field with the ball. Tyler whistled the play dead quickly, offsides. It was fast, and the crowd roared in anger. Vlad held up his hand to them, and they quieted down. Play restarted, and Krav recovered possession. Grigore scored and the fans cheered, the victory chants of Krav returning.

But it didn't get out of control. Tyler continued to call penalties against Krav and Vuhl alike, and the score remained close, always within one goal of each other. Every time Krav scored, Vuhl would battle back and keep it tight. Mark stayed true to his word and called everything he saw, even issuing a yellow card against a Krav player.

With every penalty against Krav, Vlad would raise his hand. The crowd would roar in anger, they would boo, and hiss, and spit, but they ultimately remained calm. Vlad was holding them back. But why?

Tyler tried to put it out of his mind and focused on the match. Vuhl was good, and with both Tyler and Mark giving them fair calls, they competed with Krav. Krav couldn't stomp them into the ground either, and so the score was much closer than it would be otherwise. And Tyler felt the game again. As he ran along the field, watching play, he remembered why he loved football. It was a wonderful day, and with both teams challenging each other, some great plays happened from both sides. It was real football, not the death sport that it typically was in Krav. It was beautiful.

Halftime came and went, and the score remained close. Vlad continued to hold back the Krav faithful. With five minutes left to play, a Vuhl striker broke through the Krav defenders with the ball and scored, tying the game. A tie would ruin Krav's chances at promotion for the season, and the crowd screamed for blood. Mark looked at Tyler with some concern. Tyler stood firm, shaking his head. Straight down the middle.

It was tied, and then Grigore took the team on his back. The big team of Krav was tired, their speed declining as the game went on. Their lungs were giving up on them. But Grigore wouldn't let them lose, and summoned an ungodly burst of athleticism, stealing the ball from a Vuhl striker, and taking it the length of the field, cutting hard, back and forth, before scoring with just under a minute to go in regulation.

The chants of Krav rose to dizzying heights, and the field exploded with color. The rest of Krav FC summoned the last of their energy, and they shut down Vuhl. Krav won 4-3. The crowd celebrated. Two more victories, and they would be promoted. Krav would once again be in the sun.

Tyler and Mark hurried along, just the same. Tyler doubted they'd forget the penalties or yellow card called against the team, and so they returned to their apartment while they still could. The pair dressed and rushed back, their hoods drawn down over their faces. The town was raucous in victory. Tyler bet Maria was busy at Bautura. Whatever Vlad's plan was, Krav won, fair and square.

"Christ," said Mark, collapsing into the couch.

Tyler, despite being exhausted, paced. There was still an excitement in him. It was what good football did to him. The adrenaline flowed through him, and he peeked out their window, onto Ofranda Road. Krav fans milled about, walking back and forth, shouting, singing, and celebrating.

Mark popped open a beer and turned on the television.

"That was a good game," said Tyler.

"You're right," said Mark. "It was." He took a swallow of beer. "I know why Vlad made you lead official."

"Why is that?" asked Tyler.

"He's testing you," said Mark. "He sees something in you."

"Did I pass?" asked Tyler.

"I don't know," said Mark. "You'll have to ask Vlad."

The door shook, someone knocking heavily three times.

They both jumped. Tyler opened it. It was Raul and Iosef, again. They spoke to Mark in Romanian.

"What does he want now?" asked Tyler. "Another meeting?"

Mark got up, heading for the door. Tyler moved to follow him.

"No, Tyler," said Mark. "Just me."

"Why just you?" asked Tyler.

"I don't know," said Mark. "But I'm sure it'll be more good news."

Mark left with Raul and Iosef. Tyler waited for Mark to return, but hours passed, and he was still gone.

Then the familiar chanting started again, the town singing as one, this time the triumphant victory march, as the red river flowed down Ofranda Road. Tyler sat at the window and watched as they approached. He had to watch.

Tyler felt Krav, connected to his pulse. It grew stronger and stronger as they passed, dozens at a time. He was linked to Krav, and he didn't know why or how, but he could feel it, feel the ceremony. He saw no faces, only red hoods, shadows and the night obscuring every face. Except one.

Much like Dario, there was one face not hidden, not dressed in a red robe at all, carried along in the tide.

It was Mark.

20

They had Mark. They would kill him.

Mark looked up into Tyler's eyes. The same desperate fear in Dario's eyes was there. A plea for help. But then they carried him away, pushed along by the mass of followers.

Tyler had to do something. But what? There were hundreds of them. He couldn't just barge in and take Mark. They'd overpower him.

The red robe. He stole it from the Stone House. He ran to his bag and pulled out the crimson bundle. He threw it on and looked in the mirror. The hood hung low over his face, and he was indistinguishable from any of the other faithful. Now to join them.

He left the apartment and sneaked out to the side alley which connected to the road that went to the field. The river still flowed by, the crowd slowly but inexorably marching toward the pitch. They all looked forward, and he pressed against the side of the alley until he was next to the throng. He slid in line with them as they passed the entrance, and he was with them. No one uttered a word, and he joined the chant, matching the tone of his neighbor as best he could.

He had heard the song dozens of times. He didn't understand the words, but he could replicate the sounds phonetically well enough, and he sang along with the crowd. The victory song filled the town, and Tyler became a part of it. A part of the song and a part of Krav.

Tyler had been a witness to the red river multiple times now, but he had never been inside of it, never a drop in the tide. As the song filled the air and the thousand feet of the faithful stomped the cobblestone road, it echoed in his bones and reverberated in his blood. The hymn soared and rumbled, the joined voices of thousands all roaring for Krav. The song was nothing but sound to Tyler. He was only mimicking the fans, parroting back what he had heard a dozen times. But then it wasn't just sound anymore. As he sang, the words found purchase in his throat and in his lungs, and he knew the meaning.

Beautiful, beautiful Krav
You breathe and live in us
Infinite and momentous
Glorious and unbreakable
Our blood will flow through you
You will live forever
You will live forever
You will live forever

He sang louder and louder, until he shouted the words with everyone, and he could feel Krav beneath his feet, feel her heartbeat inside him. He was with them now, and Krav had welcomed him into the fold. She knew him, and she embraced him.

Krav will conquer
Krav will defeat
Victorious, victorious Krav
The great and glorious beast
She will break the world
You will live forever
You will live forever
You will live forever

He felt the blood now. Felt the gallons of blood spilled in her name over the centuries. He saw them in his mind's eye as he marched, the decrepit road underneath his feet, the shadow of the hood covering his eyes. He felt the others around him, felt them singing with them, and shared their blood. They were the same. They knew each other as brothers and sisters of Krav. They sang together.

There is no end to her
Waiting beneath the earth
To swallow us all whole
Great and glorious Krav
Swallow us whole
You will live forever
You will live forever
You will live forever

His throat ached now from the singing. He couldn't stop, even as his lungs hurt and his throat gave out, he couldn't stop singing. The frenzy of the red river had taken him and oh god, he could feel her, feel the Great Beast that was Krav, the entity they fed, and they fed it and it pleased her and she returned the favor with victory and strength. George was wrong, George was wrong, George was wrong. She wanted the blood, wanted the death. It sustained her, had sustained her for hundreds, no, thousands of years, every sacrifice, every murder, every ounce of pain and misery, of Grigore beating a man in the street, of every stillbirth, she took it all, and consumed it, the great and glorious Krav; she will live forever.

The song repeated, and they marched slowly toward the pitch. Tyler sang with them, feeling Krav, the same as when Dario died, when he bled on the hillside. Krav was with them now. He wasn't alone. She was there for him, with him, to give him strength and power. Tyler knew that all of them felt that. All who marched felt Krav inside. She had secreted her way in, their weak defenses quickly breached by her insidious warmth.

Wake up Tyler.

Tyler!

He shook his head and broke free from the enchantment the shared singing had set upon him and looked up. They approached the pitch. He needed to get closer to Mark and figure out a way to escape the crowd.

Tyler walked forward, slowly, moving up the ranks as fast as he could without getting undue attention. If anyone in the crowd noticed him getting closer and closer to Mark, they said nothing. He peeked over the congregation, using his height to his advantage. Mark's head stuck out from the middle of the procession. It grew tighter as Tyler pushed farther up, tightly packed, shoulder to shoulder. He could force his way in, but they would notice him. It'd be a death sentence. An outsider, taking part in their ritual? Trying to disrupt it, even? They'd tear him limb from limb.

Still, he moved up. Tyler slid his body into tight spaces, keeping his head down. Everyone sang, and Tyler sang with them, but only the sounds now.

Don't say the words, Tyler, or they'll take you away again. She'll be inside you, and you'll be inside her.

And so he didn't sing the words, only the sounds, only the melody, and he moved up, and he could see Mark. The back of Mark's head, ten feet ahead of him. So close.

The bodies overlapped even tighter here. They guarded Mark, making sure he kept walking. Mark couldn't run if he wanted to, and if he tried to break free from the crowd, a dozen people would hold him and drag him along. So he walked, because he had no choice. There was nowhere else for Tyler to go without making a scene. He'd have to wait until they settled on the field, where maybe he could make a move.

They were there, the pitch in front of them, the gate at the corner unlocked and open for them, ready for the red river to flow inside. Krav flowed stronger here and Tyler could feel it, even without singing. The crowd filled the field, walking toward the center of the grass. Toward the split circle. They propelled Mark forward, his feet moving as fast as they could as the throng pushed him into the split circle. They surrounded him. The fans filled in around him, and Tyler moved as forward as he could, on the outer edge of the split circle, just behind the front line of followers, who lined the white chalk outline that formed the center of the field.

Mark stood in the center of them, inside the split circle. Mark was a hard man, but he couldn't hide the fear in his eyes. They had taken him, and they would kill him. Why Mark? Why now?

The procession still flowed in behind him, taking up the entire field. The red overtook the green grass, black in the darkness. Soon, nothing but red surrounded him and Mark.

A voice spoke, then, yelled, and the chanting and singing stopped. Everyone stood silent. The word was in Romanian, but Tyler understood it, somehow. He was connected to Krav, and all the Krav faithful spoke a single language, one that was rooted into the earth, underneath the surface.

"<Victory!>" yelled the voice. Tyler recognized it. It was Vlad's.

The crowd echoed back the shout.

A figure in a red robe stepped into the split circle with Mark. His face remained in shadow, but he was the rough size and shape of Vlad, obscured slightly by the robe. The crowd silenced itself, waiting for Vlad to talk.

"<We join together here after another victory,>" said Vlad. "<A hard-fought victory, but a victory nonetheless.>"

The crowd cheered again.

"<And today we will honor the split circle and deliver unto Krav a blessing,>" said Vlad. "<And also deliver a punishment, and a message to all those who within our ranks who would disrespect us, and disrespect Krav.>"

The figure reached into his robe and pulled out a dagger, short and sharp. The moonlight glinted off the blade.

"<Mark here has been a part of our community for

years,>" said Vlad. "<He has lived, eaten and drank, and worked with us. He has been with us since the new beginning, since we witnessed Krav reborn. And he has been loyal, and we accepted him in our midst because of that fact. It is a great honor to be welcomed into Krav, as an outsider, as a foreigner. Very few have been given that respect. And yet he betrayed us!>"

The dagger went up Mark's throat. Mark stood there, his arms by his sides, tense. His eyes were on Vlad, full of fear, and sadness, and anger, roiling around inside him.

"What are you doing, mate?" asked Mark. "It doesn't have to be like this. You saved my life."

"<Even now he tries to negotiate for his life,>" said Vlad. "<He tries to get back into our good graces. Into Krav's good graces. But he can't blind us anymore to his treacherous ways. He tried to ensure a loss today. But he failed. As all will fail against Krav, may she live forever.>"

"<She will live forever,>" chanted the crowd in return.

Vlad was working his flock, making them think Mark was responsible for the day's officiating. It worked. The congregation wanted his blood. And Vlad would give it to them. Give it to Krav.

"You're gonna kill me?" asked Mark. "For this phony religion? After all we've been through together? I thought you were better than this. I stayed here with you because I thought you were better."

Vlad spoke now, but in English, and only to Mark. The first few rows of people could hear, but he wasn't announcing this. He only needed Mark to hear.

"We're too close now, brother," said Vlad. "It's almost time. And you were getting in the way. I can't risk it, not from anyone. Even you. You cannot protect him. Do not worry. You will live forever inside of Krav."

"You're insane! All of you!" yelled Mark. "It's just football. It's just a game. Look what you're doing. You're bleeding men down to the bone for a game!" Spittle was flying from his mouth as he screamed at the impassive followers.

They would not be swayed.

The crowd remained silent, and Mark saw him then, his eyes latched onto Tyler's. It silenced him, and the same look of terrible fear and dread was there, tears rolling down from his eyes. Mark said nothing.

"<Grab him,>" said Vlad, and hooded figures emerged from the pack, each taking a limb, and holding him stationary. Another large figure came from behind him, putting an arm around his neck. It could only be Grigore. There was no one else that size.

"<For Krav!>" yelled Vlad, and the crowd echoed him. Mark cried now, screaming.

Vlad ran the dagger through one arm, deeply cutting him from wrist to armpit. The dagger slid easily through Mark's flesh.

He did the same on the other. Blood poured from Mark's arm, coming down in torrents onto the field.

Vlad bent down and did the same with his legs, from the Achilles to his ass, the dagger cutting deep.

He did the other leg. The blood poured out of him. Tyler had never seen so much blood.

Mark screamed with every slice, crying and pleading for his life.

"Please, Vlad, please, mate," said Mark.

"Shh," said Vlad. Grigore grabbed Mark's thinning hair

and pulled his head back.

Vlad drew the dagger across Mark's neck, silencing him, blood flowing freely. Grigore pushed the dying body of Mark forward and he crumpled onto the split circle.

Tyler watched it all happen and did nothing.

21

After Mark died, and bled all the blood he had, they carried his body back to the Stone House.

Tyler didn't interfere. He stood and waited with the crowd. He followed their lead, chanting and singing as they did. The connection to Krav still thrummed, but he segmented it away. The horror of what he had seen was too much, and it kept his mind his own. He didn't let Krav in.

The red river would return to the Stone House, leaving the football field, going back the way they came. The faithful continued to sing and chant. They had been victorious in all ways today. The game had ended in a Krav win, and they had extinguished a voice of dissent in making an offering to Krav herself.

Vlad's words rang through his mind as they walked into

town. "You can't protect him." He had been talking about Tyler. Mark had said it often enough. Told Tyler time and time again, that he could only defend him so much. But he had, Tyler realized. He had protected him from the very beginning, and continued right until the end, letting Tyler's identity as one of the red robes remain secret. And Tyler had returned it with inaction. He had watched Mark die.

But now he had no protection. He needed to get out of Krav. There was no saving this place, no salvaging the purity of football here. He would get out and find the proper authorities. They could come in and dig up the bodies. He had to escape. He would talk to Maria.

As the procession left the field and walked back into town, Tyler joined them and ducked into the alley he had first emerged from, next to his apartment, slipping inside. He took off the red robe and stuffed it deep in his bag. Just holding it in his hands made him feel nauseous.

Mark was dead, fuck, they cut him apart, right in front of you, and you did nothing, Tyler, you stood there and let it happen. He was protecting you and you let it happen.

Mark wouldn't be drinking any more beer while he watched TV, or joining you at Bautura tonight. He wouldn't be doing anything because he was already starting to rot, and they'd bury him in an unmarked grave somewhere in Krav, and Krav would have the rest of him. The bile in Tyler's guts roiled, and then surged up into his throat, and he leaned over the sink and threw up stomach acid, burning his mouth and nose.

He spit it all out and drank some water from the tap, cupping it with his hand. He sunk down onto the kitchen floor and started sobbing. The fear, the horror, the frustration had built up inside him for weeks now, and it came bursting out of him. He cried without thought. Time passed, and his tears subsided. They didn't have time for sorrow. He found a tissue and blew his nose. He washed his face. He needed to get to Maria and get them both out of town.

He looked outside. The red river had run its course, flowing up Ofranda Road, back into the Stone House. Tyler left, his pace brisk. Maria was the only thing on his mind. He would talk to her, tell her what had happened to Mark, and escape. Tonight, if possible.

As he approached Maria's home, he sneaked around to the side, looking inside for any sign of trouble or visitors. He didn't know if Vlad was watching her or not. After George's explanation of Krav's power, he wasn't sure if it mattered. But he looked anyway. He knocked softly on the back door. No reply. It was unlocked, and he went in. The house was quiet, and as he walked through the kitchen, he picked up a frying pan for good measure.

They could already be here.

He raised the pan up to shoulder level, ready to attack anyone.

He went into the tiny living room. Maria slept on the couch, game shows flickering on the television. The floor creaked beneath him loudly, and her eyes fluttered open to see him, and she yelped, sitting bolt upright.

"It's me, it's me," said Tyler, lowering the pan.

"Christ, Tyler," said Maria, catching her breath. "You scared the shit out of me."

"I didn't know if your dad had anyone here with you," said Mark.

"No, not yet, thankfully," said Maria. "He seems to think

I'll just go along with whatever he says. Are you okay?"

"No," said Tyler, sitting down next to her, his head in his hands. "I am far from okay. He killed him, Maria. Your father. Right in front of me. Right in front of me!"

"Slow down," said Maria, putting an arm around him. Tyler caught himself. He had to remain calm if he would convince her of this. "What happened?"

"You saw the game?" asked Tyler.

"Yes," said Maria. "From my father's seats."

"They came after," said Tyler. "Your father's henchmen. They took Mark, and he was taken by the red robes, just like Dario. I sneaked in with them. I wore a red robe. They took him to mid-field, and your father butchered him in the middle of the football field!"

"I don't believe it," she said.

"And I did nothing," said Tyler. "I let it happen. I lectured him, Maria. I lectured Mark about doing nothing in this town, and I let him get killed."

Maria's face was conflicted, her eyes darting back and forth.

"Are you sure?" asked Maria.

"Yes, I"m sure," said Tyler. "You don't think I can't recognize your father by now? He called Mark a traitor in front of the whole town, and then sliced him open with a dagger. They took his body."

"They were best friends, Tyler," said Maria. "My father wouldn't kill him. It's impossible."

"I saw it with my own eyes," said Tyler. "We need to get out of town. Tonight."

"What?" asked Maria. "Leave? Now?"

"Yes," said Tyler. "We talked about this. It's not safe here anymore, and there's nothing we can do about it. We're only two people, and the whole town is complicit. We have to go find some authorities. Government officials. Interpol. Somebody."

"What will happen to my father?" asked Maria.

"He'll get arrested and go to prison," said Tyler. "He's a killer, Maria."

"I'll never see him again," said Maria. "I'll lose him."

"You've already lost him," said Tyler. "Whatever he's become, he's not the man you used to know."

"Or maybe he's always been this man," said Maria. She covered her face and started to cry, her shoulders shaking. Tyler put his arm over her, holding her.

"I--I'm sorry, I know this must be hard on you. It's your own father--"

"No, you're right," she said. "It's not safe here anymore. I should have seen the signs from the beginning. But I ignored them, looked the other way. I always have with him. He's all I've had since mother passed. He's all there was for me. And then we moved, and if it wasn't true before, it became true then. He was my anchor. And we settled here in Krav, and he showed me it, and-"

She flinched then, her face contorting for a moment. She blinked, over and over.

"Maria?" he asked. "Are you okay?"

"Yes yes yes no no, please help me," she said. It looked like she was having a stroke. "He did it, the prophecy, and I can't come back, Krav, she--"

She flinched again, grabbing her head between her two hands, squeezing it hard between her palms. She grunted in pain, her eyes closed tight.

"Unngh," she said.

"Maria!" he said. "What's happening?"

She exhaled, all the breath leaving her body, and then breathed in deep.

"Talk to me," said Tyler. "Are you okay?"

"I'm okay," she said, gasping for air. "I don't know what happened."

"Do you feel alright?" asked Tyler.

"I do now," she said. "Something passed over me."

"It looked like you were having a stroke, or a panic attack. You're sure you're okay?" he asked.

"Yes," said Maria. "I feel fine now. Back to normal. What was I saying?"

"Something about Krav?" asked Tyler. "About your father showing you it."

She nodded, looking Tyler in the eyes. "Yes. He showed me Krav." She paused. "You're right. We need to leave. Leave Krav behind. Make a clean break. Get out of the town, away from my father's grasp."

"Let's throw your stuff together and get moving--"

"But not tonight," said Maria.

"What? Why?" he asked.

"Everyone is here," said Maria. "They are probably watching the house right now. They will leave the Stone House shortly, and spread back out through town. We don't have time." She grabbed his hand. Her impossible golden touch.

She was right.

"Then when?"

"The next away game," she said. "The town will be deserted. We will have time to pack, to prepare." She paused. "And I will get a chance to say goodbye to my father."

"It's a risk," he said.

"It's a risk either way," she said. "A clean break."

"A clean break."

"But promise me. Promise you won't leave Krav without me," she said. "I--I love you, Tyler." She looked away and then back. "I feel like a child, saying that, but it is true. Promise me you won't leave me here."

"I love you too," he said, kissing her. "I promise. We will leave Krav together."

22

Tyler and Maria stayed quiet and prepared. They got bug-out bags ready, and Maria prepped her Jeep for their escape.

Tyler kept his eyes open for any changes. He didn't notice any surveillance, but if what George said was true, Vlad wouldn't need any. Krav would tell him all he needs to know. But he couldn't do anything if he was out of town. Krav needed their final two victories. Vlad wouldn't endanger that.

Tyler felt the anxiety build inside him as the time ticked by. By the morning of the next away game, he worried the ball of worry would eat him alive. Still, he had to keep up appearances.

George remained the same, speaking loudly about his complaints about Krav, as if Tyler had just started working there. George compartmentalized it all. The surface level of Krav over here, in this part of his mind, the horror underneath over here. Vlad's murders sectioned away, something not to be discussed. But he was not surprised when, over lunch, Tyler told him he was leaving Krav.

"She is not your home," said George. They hadn't talked about Mark's death. Tyler assumed George knew. "I didn't expect you to stay for so long. No one stays."

"You stayed," said Tyler. "You've lived here your whole life."

"Yes," said George. "And see what that has done for me." He gestured around them. "I have my shop. And my dumplings."

"They are damn good dumplings," said Tyler. "Best I've ever had."

"You are kind," said George. "But I sometimes question why I stay."

"You could come with us," said Tyler.

"You are taking Maria?" asked George, nodding. "That is smart. She deserves more than Krav, more than her father. But I cannot leave. It is too late for that. Much too late. When Vlad left, that was my chance. He opened the door for me, and I let it swing shut."

"You thought he was a traitor," said Tyler. "A coward."

"I speak loudly, don't I?" asked George, with a slight smile. "But as much as I dislike him, I can understand his choices. We were friends. We faced similar decisions. At crucial junctures, Vlad took the easier path, time after time. I took the hard road. Does that make him cowardly? Or does it just make me stupid?"

"You're one of the smartest men I've ever met," said Tyler.

"Do not say that," said George. "I have made too many mistakes in my life to be considered a smart man."

"A smart man learns from his mistakes," said Tyler. "And doesn't repeat them."

George met his eyes then and nodded. He sighed. "You are right. Promise me you'll protect Maria. I have grown an affection for that young woman."

"She doesn't need my help," said Tyler.

"No," said George. "That is certain. She is strong, and smart, but still, you must take care of her. Like it or not, she has the blood of Krav in her veins. If the legacy of this town will carry on, it will be because of her."

The memory of her episode the night before flashed through Tyler's mind and then was gone.

"I promise," said Tyler. "I shouldn't have said anything."

"You are an open book to me, Tyler," said George. "You are easy to read."

"Like I said, you're a smart guy," said Tyler. "Sure you don't want to come with us?"

"I presume you will call the authorities down on Krav?" asked George. "On Vlad?"

Tyler paused. "Yes," he said, finally.

"And you think they will find something?" asked George.

"I think so," said Tyler. "No matter how well he hides the bodies."

"What will happen to Krav?" asked George.

"I don't know," said Tyler. "I imagine their football team will face some problems. Vlad will be arrested, I hope."

"Then the town will need leadership," said George. "If it is to survive at all. I do not want Krav to die, Tyler. I would do anything to keep her alive. And if I must stay to do that,

that is what I will do."

"But there's so much more out there," said Tyler. "There's more in this world than Krav."

"Did you know I was married once?" asked George.

"I didn't," said Tyler. "What happened?"

George said nothing for a moment. "She died."

"I'm sorry to hear that," said Tyler.

"I would say that it is okay, that I am over it," said George. "But I am not. I have never gotten over it. I got through it, if that makes sense. She was an amazing woman. She was the best of us. Strong and smart. Like Maria. And beautiful. So beautiful. I couldn't fathom why a woman who looked like that would spend time with an ogre like myself. Her hair. Long and black. Perfect. But she did."

Tyler had never seen George like this. All the tension and worry he carried with him like an Atlas stone had vanished. He glanced away, his mind transporting him somewhere else. He looked happy.

"This was under the worst of Stroescu's rule. Always worrying about food shortages, about secret police. But none of it mattered to us. We were young and in love. Despite all the pain, all the worry, we had each other. We got married. What a beautiful day. I can still remember the sun, the breeze. The dancing. Time passed. But then Vlad left, and things began to change."

"Like what?" asked Tyler.

"Vlad bore the responsibility back then, being so talented at football, of being the face of Krav. It might have been why he left. That, and to get out from under Stroescu. But he had been pegged as the next leader of Krav. And I didn't mind it. He was my friend. He was capable. The people respected him. But when he left..."

"It fell to you," said Tyler.

"Yes," said George. "And given control of the future of the town, I came to realize that Krav was not worth the toll of blood we were exacting. I changed things. I ended the bloodshed. That decision, and my decision to become the steward of Krav--it forced my hand. There were repercussions I couldn't foresee. By eliminating the sacrifices. And I had to choose between Krav and my wife."

"You chose Krav," said Tyler.

"Like I said," said George. "I would do anything for Krav. And ultimately, it killed my Elena. She couldn't bear it."

"You don't have to still live under the shadow of that," said Tyler. "It can be forgotten."

"No, it cannot," said George. "Krav remembers. She will not forget my decision, and she will not forget me. I must remain here, Tyler. I must ensure that Krav survives. I have invested everything in her."

"I thought--I thought that football was everything to me. But it's not. It's still a beautiful game, but it is not more important than people."

"Not a believer anymore?" asked George.

"Not enough," said Tyler. "Not enough to stay and fight a losing battle for it. Krav can have its football, but I want no part of it."

"You will not hear me defend the game," said George. "If that's what you're waiting for."

"I know, I know," said Tyler. "But it has been my life since I was a child. Everything else ignored, pushed aside for it. After I leave Krav, after this is settled, what do I do? I have no career to return to."

"You could stay," said George. "Settle into Vlad's pocket. He likes you. He wants you."

"I can't," said Tyler.

"And that's why you're a good person," said George. "Maybe not smart, but good. You take the hard road. Like me."

They finished lunch and got back to work. As they worked, Tyler knew the town was leaving, little by little, following the buses carrying Krav FC to their final away game. Krav would face the worst team in Level 4, a game they would most likely win. He tried to push the thoughts of the night ahead of him aside, but they intruded nonetheless.

Not only that, but the question of what comes after. After they escape, what will he do? Will he go back to Portland, and become a car salesman? What will happen to Maria, and to Bautura? Will she still want to remain in Krav, after her father is removed?

Focus, Tyler. None of that has happened yet. Worry about tonight.

One step at a time. They needed to get out of town and to the authorities. He had Maria with him, and she would help. She anchored him. She would carry him through all of this.

Before he left George's shop behind for good, George embraced him and held him tight. George hadn't hugged him before. He'd barely shown any physical affection at all. But he embraced him now, and Tyler returned it.

"Thank you for your help," said George. "And for eating my dumplings."

"It was great working with you, George," said Tyler. "Thank you for everything."

Tyler went to leave. George stopped him. "Tyler." Tyler

turned back.

"I wish you the best of luck," said George. "I hope you can leave Krav behind. It is something I've never been able to do."

23

All of Krav was at the game. Maria was right, it was a perfect time to escape.

Tyler grabbed his bag, taking one last look around the apartment. It only reminded him of Mark. He had gone through Mark's things and taken some valuables for safe-keeping. Whatever happened to them, he didn't want them to end up with Vlad. Vlad had stolen enough from Mark.

The town was empty as he walked up Ofranda Road to Maria's home. He expected someone to step out of the shadows and grab him. But no one stopped him on the way, and he found her in her house, shoving the last of her things into a duffel bag.

"Are you ready to go?" he asked.

"No," she said. "But I will go, anyway. This is our best chance. I said goodbye to my father, before he left. He doesn't know that it will be the last time I see him."

"He deserves nothing better," said Tyler.

"You're right," she said. "Let's go."

She hoisted the bag over her shoulder, and then doubled over, and then fell to a knee, the bag thumping on the floor. She grabbed her head again.

She groaned and grunted.

"Maria," he said, by her side.

"Leave me--leave Tyler," she said, the words struggling to come out of her mouth. "You--you c--c--can't h--have--"

She squeezed her skull between her hands, her fingers pressing deep into her skin. He clutched her wrists and tried to pull her off of herself, but it didn't work. Her grip tightened like a vice. She grunted, gasping for breath.

"No," she said and then her grip softened, and she pulled her hands away. Her skin was still marked, dark red where her fingers had pressed in.

"Maria, talk to me," he said.

"I'm okay," she said. "I think Krav is doing something to me."

"You mean your father is doing something to you," said Tyler. "He's turning her against you."

"I don't know," she said. "It feels like there's someone else trying to take over."

"We need to get out of town, now more than ever. It's this place," he said. "Let's go."

She nodded, and they carried the last of her things to the jeep, parked in the alley behind the house. Maria pulled off a tarp and revealed the vehicle loaded with luggage, boxes, and bags.

"I've grabbed a lot of supplies," she said. "I don't know where we'll end up, necessarily. Heading for the capitol is our best bet. The airport there can get us anywhere in Europe. The federal police are there as well."

"Better to be prepared," said Tyler.

They got into the jeep, Maria behind the wheel. She expertly reversed it in the tight alley and drove out onto Ofranda Road. They passed the apartment, and the road that led to the pitch and the split circle. They were leaving.

Not that long ago that Tyler had been riding into town, in that van, his head screaming. Seeing Krav for the first time. Meeting Mark. It felt like an eternity ago, and Portland a past life.

That's what it was now. An old life, made obsolete by the new one, and new beliefs. He couldn't go back. He would forge something new. Maria sped up as they got farther away from the center of town, avoiding the potholes as much as she could. Small farms and houses passed by on their right and left in the dark. There were no lights on. Everyone had traveled to the game.

Until there were some. Dancing in front of them, far down the road. Red lights flickered at the edge of their vision.

"What is that?" asked Tyler.

"Something's wrong," said Maria.

She slowed the jeep down. They soon saw the source of light. A set of flares burned away on the rough asphalt. They cast brilliant reds into the air. Tyler had to shield his eyes as they approached, the headlights revealing what the flares marked. A tractor blocked the road, a large one. The road itself was only wide enough for one vehicle, and the length of the tractor crossed the entire width of the pavement, spilling over onto the meager shoulders before they dropped off into rocky dips. The terrain on the side was impossible to pass, even with a jeep. Piles of jagged rocks lined the highway, and where there weren't rocks, there were rows of thin, dense trees, thick enough to deter anything.

Two men stood next to the tractor.

"What the hell are they doing out here?" asked Maria. "Driving a tractor in the dark."

"They knew we were coming," said Tyler. "It's a blockade. After everyone left." Maria came to a stop, putting the jeep in park.

"What do we do?" asked Maria.

As they sat there, twenty feet from the tractor, the two men turned to stare at them.

"Maria," said Tyler, pointing. "Turn around. Now."

Suddenly, from behind the tractor, another man rose from the shadows. And then another. And another. It was a fucking ambush.

"Is there any other way out of town?" asked Tyler.

They were approaching the jeep now. They carried hammers, clubs, and scythes.

"The only bridge is this way," she said. "There's no way to cross the river. The jeep would never make it across."

"Come on, there has to be another way," said Tyler. They were close. They walked toward them.

"There's a granite path to the west, but it's a horse trail. It's narrow," she said. "It eventually leads to a bridge, but it's out in the middle of nowhere."

"Who cares," he said. "Go go go." She slammed the jeep

in reverse, and floored it, kicking up the dust in the road, doing a quick 180 and speeding back the other direction, into the center of town.

"They knew. They knew!" yelled Tyler. "You can't keep secrets in Krav."

"This is my fault," she said. "We should have left earlier, we should--"

"It's too late for that. Let's get to the path, and figure it out from there. Could we possibly get out on foot?"

"I mean, maybe," she said. "But there's nothing except fields and rocks for dozens of kilometers in any direction. There's nowhere to hide."

"Fuck," said Tyler. "I hope that path is wide enough."

They roared back through Krav, going much faster than they should. The town still seemed empty, but Tyler didn't know anymore. He envisioned eyes in every house, staring at him, reporting on him. Krav was watching. George had told him, but he hadn't really believed.

They sped through the center of town and turned west, and then passed it, speeding up even more. Tyler had never been this direction, but it looked much like the rest of Krav. It petered out quicker than driving south toward the bridge.

Soon the road turned to gravel, and Tyler understood why Maria was so hesitant to go this way. The path was just wide enough for the jeep to drive on. On each side there was a sharp incline that fell over ten feet. If the jeep went too far to either side, it would be gone, rolling over. In the dark, the headlights only showed the dusty gravel road, a stark line of white in front of them, with two huge chasms on both sides. Maria had to slow to a crawl.

"We're sitting ducks up here," said Tyler.

"It's the only way out," said Maria.

"Do your best," said Tyler, and they crawled along the path. The jeep inched along, the tires crunching over the gravel, each tire on the outside edge of the thin trail. Tyler's heart beat hard in his chest, but it was Maria he worried about. If she had another episode, they'd fall. He readied himself to grab the steering wheel, if that would do any good at all.

"How long does it continue like this?" he said.

"A long time," she said. "I don't think many use it anymore."

They moved slowly, but they made progress, and Tyler saw no lights behind them. They weren't being followed. If they were patient, they would get out.

But then he saw another light ahead of them, and unlike the flares, he recognized it right away. They drove up to it, but it was plain what it was.

Bales of hay sat in the middle of the path, stacked a dozen deep. They burned, a blaze soaring up into the sky. The path was blocked. He knew they were heavy, and even if they could move them, they would burn for hours.

"We're trapped," she said. "They've trapped us."

"Let's go back," he said.

"I can't," she said. "I can't take the jeep backwards down this thing. We'll fall off." Tyler eyed the side of the road. It was precarious enough going forward, but in reverse? Impossible.

"Then we walk," he said. "We face them, head on."

Maria cried then, soft tears that she didn't wipe away. The frustration welled up in Tyler's chest, and he lashed out, hammering the dashboard with fists.

"Fuck!" he yelled, his face red. He wanted to scream, but what good would it do. Tyler stopped, finally, his hands aching. He reached over and wiped away her tears.

"We will get out of this," he said. "Together." He kissed her then, and she kissed back, deep and loving, gentle, warm. "I love you."

"I love you," she said and they forced themselves out of the jeep, each shouldering their biggest bag, grabbing flashlights. They started back down the gravel road, silently. They didn't know what they would find in Krav, but they walked, their feet clattering the old broken rock. They held hands as they walked back into Krav.

Eventually they got to the edge of town. A parked SUV sat there, idling, its headlights aimed right at them. As they approached, multiple figures emerged from it. Tyler saw two of them, clear as day. Vlad and Grigore. They hadn't gone to the game. Tyler and Maria continued toward them. There was no other way. Vlad smiled.

"Did you really think Krav would let you leave, just as she needs you most?"

24

Tyler sat in his apartment again. He'd thought he had left it behind.

They had separated him and Maria. Vlad took her back to her house, while Grigore and a few other Vlad henchmen escorted Tyler to the apartment. Tyler didn't resist. They would beat him to a pulp just for fun. He would play Vlad's game, whatever it was.

"Running away, little chicken?" asked Grigore. Grigore stood above him, towered over him, with Tyler sitting on the couch.

"I'm not the one who left his team to play without him," said Tyler. "So that he could be bossed around by a has-been."

Grigore laughed. "You have been here for how long?

Weeks? A month? And you still do not know the sport here. We played Kalpa. They are joke. Terrible, every year. Half of team is children or old men. Krav did not need me there to beat them." His face grew serious. "And you should not insult Coach. He is great man."

"He's a killer," said Tyler. "He's made you a killer. You could leave Krav. You don't have to do this. You're a good player, you could play anywhere--"

"You do not pay attention," said Grigore. "Krav is home. And everything we do is to honor her. Coach saved me. He gave me purpose, understand? I was wild dog, running where my mind led me. Now, I exist for Krav. I work for her. I live for her."

"Your great man fled Krav, just like I was trying to do. He only came back when he had no other choices."

Grigore smiled, that shark tooth grin. "You are trying to rile me, little chick. No man is perfect. He came back, that is important. He came back to help. He saw what he did was wrong and returned, doing right thing. Doing right thing for Krav. You will see. I have faith. Now be quiet. I don't want to have to hurt you. Coach will be here soon."

He wasn't, though. Hours went by, and Vlad didn't show. The night wore on until the early morning. Finally, Vlad appeared, coming into the apartment like he owned the place. Technically, he did.

Grigore nodded as Vlad came in. Tyler ignored him. He sat on the couch, watching television.

Vlad spoke to Grigore in Romanian, and they had a brief exchange, before Vlad took his attention to Tyler. Vlad sat in the easy chair next to the couch. Tyler ignored him still, staring at the TV. He didn't particularly care about what was on, but he didn't want to give Vlad the satisfaction. Vlad looked at him, waiting, before finally turning it off with the remote control. Tyler slowly turned his eyes to Vlad.

"I was watching that," said Tyler.

"Very funny," said Vlad.

"Someone has to be the smart-ass after you murdered Mark," said Tyler, staring Vlad dead in the eyes. "Pick up the slack, you know?"

"I'm sure I have no idea what you're talking about," said Vlad. "Mark left town in the middle of the night. He was fixing games, you see. Big scandal."

"Seems to be a lot of people trying to leave," said Tyler. "Dario, Mark, me and your daughter. You, even! Must say something about Krav, that everyone wants to get the fuck out. Man, you must have really run out of options if you came back to this shithole--"

"Enough," said Vlad. "I will not stand by and listen to your petulance. Maria piles it on top of me, I do not need it from you as well."

"You still consider her your child?" asked Tyler. "I'd think you throw her under the bus too. Anything to distract from your own sins."

"You know nothing about Maria," said Vlad. "And you should not pretend that you do. Did you think I would let you leave town with my only daughter?"

"I don't know, Vlad," said Tyler. "You're a hard man to read sometimes. I don't understand you, still. You say you want to help Krav be better, but you turn the town toward murder. You save your best friend from being hunted, but then kill him yourself. So I don't know what you would do. Maybe you'd let us leave."

"Both of you are much too important. I meant what I said. Krav needs you, Tyler. You cannot go, not yet. Maria either. You are both vital to the future of Krav," he said.

"Why on Earth would I help you when you're kidnapping me?" asked Tyler. "When you're keeping me from Maria?"

"I see your potential, Tyler," said Vlad. "I see what you can become, and what you can do for Krav. We've had a lot of men come through Krav, and none of them have been like you. You want to see Maria? Cooperate, and I won't stand in your way. In fact, I'd encourage you. I don't want to kidnap you. I want you to stay of your own free will."

"Why me?" asked Tyler.

"Because you're good," said Vlad. "Because you see football the same way I do. Because you *feel* Krav the same way I do. You can't lie to me, Tyler, I have felt you, connected to her. Just as I am. And that is special. She has chosen you. She has earmarked you as one vital to the cause and to her, and I cannot let you leave. She needs you. Don't tell me you haven't felt it."

"I've felt nothing but death and fear from Krav," said Tyler.

"You don't need to be ashamed, Tyler," said Vlad. "I know you've noticed it. The feeling of belonging. Your old home rejected you, framed you for a crime you didn't commit. Did anyone stand up for you? Did anyone defend you? No. They shuttled you away. No one stuck their neck out for you. Here, you can be a part of Krav. You can be a part of Krav forever."

"So I can kill my friends?" asked Tyler. "Bleed them dry after they trusted me for years?"

Vlad held a stare for a moment, and then spoke. "You did not know Mark. You did not know him as I did. Whatever he has told he has done, he has done much worse in his life. He was an animal, and I brought him back to humanity. But his nature won out. He was standing in the way of Krav. If he was my friend, he would understand how important Krav is to me, and he would help me, any way he could. But he interfered. I would do anything for Krav."

"Murder is murder," said Tyler. "And you've made the whole town complicit."

Vlad chuckled at that, an alien noise coming from him. "Oh young man," he said. "Do you know Krav?"

Tyler sensed a trick question and did not answer.

"You think you do," said Vlad. "But you do not truly know her. Not yet. I do know her. Know her very well. Why do you put this all on me? Because I am the face of Krav? Because the people have elected me to lead?"

"Who else would it be?" asked Tyler.

"Have you ever considered, even once, that I am the one holding *them* back?" asked Vlad. "Dario was young, but he was from Krav, and he failed. He understood the cost of failure. Mark was a traitor. Neither was innocent. If I was not here, do you think the amount of blood shed would be less?" He paused. "When I was a child, under Stroescu, Krav was a *slaughterhouse*. Do you understand? They were killing children. Newborns. Up in the Stone House. My baby brother was ripped from my mother's arms, and killed, squealing, to feed Krav. And you call me a killer?"

"Less blood doesn't make you sinless," said Tyler. "George proved that the town could be peaceful--"

"George doesn't understand," said Vlad. "There needs to

be a balance. That is what Krav desires. George is smart, and Krav needs him, but he doesn't understand. Not yet. Like you. You both will."

"I will do nothing to help you," said Tyler.

"You are what, American hero?" asked Vlad. "Come here to save us. To show us right and wrong?" Vlad stared at him, with his cold eyes, studying him.

"I'm not a hero," said Tyler. "And there's more than black and white. But some things are non-negotiable."

Vlad narrowed his eyes and nodded at him. There was something, behind his eyes, but Tyler couldn't read it. Vlad smiled. "You say that," said Vlad. "But I think you will do the right thing. Krav believes in you, and so do I." He stood up.

"Leaving?" asked Tyler.

"Yes," said Vlad. "I need to get some sleep. We have practice later today. Our last match is in a few days, and I need to study tape if we are to win. You should rest, it will be a tough game."

"Do you except me to officiate it by myself?" asked Tyler.

"I will give you help," said Vlad. "He will do exactly as you command."

"And I assume you want me to help Krav with the calls?" asked Tyler.

"I want you to do the right thing," said Vlad, winking at him. "We took your passport and your phone. There will be men outside. If you need food, they will bring you it. But do not leave. It would be very foolish, and they will be forced to hurt you."

And then Vlad left, without a second glance, with Grigore right behind him. The other men posted up outside the apartment door, shutting it. Tyler was left alone.

They left Tyler alone for days. It was futile to try to escape. Vlad had him. He desperately wanted to communicate with Maria, but it was impossible. Every time he looked outside, no matter what time it was, there were two men there, holding clubs. He could jump out the window, but what would that get him? Leaving town wasn't an option with no passport. And he had promised her. He wouldn't leave without Maria.

So he slept when he could. He ate the food his guards brought him, which were mostly sandwiches and chips from the local deli. They served their purpose well enough. They weren't as good as George's dumplings, but nothing was.

He only had his thoughts. They circulated in his mind, a jumbled mess of his exile from Portland, his journey to Krav, and the descent into chaos. His relationship with Maria. Mark's death, dying in front of him.

Ultimately, it all came down to a choice. Work with Vlad and help Krav win the game. Or call it down the middle and face the consequences of upsetting him. Krav may still win, even with fair calls. But they may lose and then suffer another season of being Level 4. The town may revolt. Vlad had promised them a lot, and how long could he forestall results?

If he helped them win, he would gain Vlad's favor. There'd be no more obstacles between him and Maria. He'd have his life. But what did George say, about being in Vlad's pocket? If Tyler got in there, he didn't think he would ever get out.

Vlad's way was the easy way. It ensured Tyler his life, a career, Maria.

For once in your life, go the easy way.

He looked up, and saw Mark's old kit, framed and hung on the wall.

No. If he helped Vlad, he was no better than him. Might as well have cut Mark's throat himself.

Fuck Vlad, and fuck Krav. She wasn't getting Tyler's help.

25

Time slowed down over those few days, letting Tyler's decision rest with him. It passed slowly, but it passed, and soon, it was game time.

Vlad didn't talk to him again, and he heard nothing from Maria. He assumed she would be at the match but he didn't know. He was kept in the dark. He only had the apartment.

The weather had turned to spring, and the nights were comfortable enough for Tyler to keep the windows open. In the morning before the last game of the season, he found a stone on the floor, tossed in through the window. A rubber band held a piece of paper to the rock. He opened it. Printed in neat English was a short note.

Be ready after the game. We are getting out of here. I will take care of Maria.

George

Nothing else. Maybe Tyler's words influenced George. He had to hope that George could handle his end of the plan, whatever it was.

Then they took him out of it. He knew it was coming. He could hear the town. It started buzzing before dawn. This game would decide the season. A win, and they would be promoted. It would change everything for Krav if they got moved up to a higher league. If they lost, they'd stay down in the basement of Level 4.

It wouldn't be an easy victory. They were facing Arba for the second time, the team that narrowly beat them, and led to Dario's death. Arba was fighting for the same thing, for promotion to the next level, so they wouldn't roll over for Krav. And that was with substantial help from Mark's officiating. Tyler didn't know if Krav could hang with them if he called it down the middle. It could turn into a rout early on, and then things would get ugly.

But whatever the result, it was a chance for him to separate himself from his guards. Win or lose, the arena would undoubtedly fall into chaos. He could lose them in it and get the hell out of dodge.

The thugs escorted him to the stadium, to the official's locker room. A teenage boy waited for him inside, already dressed in an ref's uniform.

"Who are you?" asked Tyler.

"I am Alexei," he said. "Hello. I am assistant official." He extended his hand, and Tyler shook it. The kid was young, with short brown hair and a lopsided, innocent grin. He was shorter than Tyler, and skinny. He smiled now.

"How good is your English?" asked Tyler.

"So so," said Alexei. He waggled his fingers back and forth in the universal symbol for sort of.

"Out there, you keep your eyes open and your mouth shut. Don't call anything unless I give you the go ahead. If you see something suspect, you tell me, and I'll make the decision. Do you understand?" asked Tyler.

"Yes," said Alexei. "Let you make calls. Keep mouth shut."

"Where are you from?" asked Tyler.

"Krav," said the kid, with the same goofy grin.

"Listen," said Tyler. "We call this down the middle. No favoring either team."

"Let you make calls. Keep mouth shut," he said, repeating himself.

"Good enough," said Tyler. "And stay away from Grigore." Just saying the name made the kid's eyes go wide, so Tyler think he knew that lesson.

Tyler changed into his uniform and waited. The thrum of the stands started again, the building shaking as the crowd began to dance and sing. He could hear the song echoing down to them, and he was back in the red river, hiding under his hood. Watching Mark die.

YOU WILL LIVE FOREVER

He tried to breathe, but the ball of nerves coiled in his gut was almost unbearable. He had never felt this before. His stomach was collapsing in on itself, and the rest of him would follow, swallowed up like a black hole. Tyler forced his eyes closed and pushed everything away. The shaking of the stadium. The victory song of Krav. Mark's pleas for mercy before his death. He shoved them aside. Maria was there, but he let her linger. They'd find a way out from this. They would escape.

Alexei startled him when he tapped him on the shoulder.

"It is game time," he said, his heavy accent coming through.

They walked out, the two thugs trailing them as they went onto the field. Tyler had to blink a few times as he looked at the pitch. It was brighter than ever.

It had fed on Mark. Krav fed, and the field prospered.

He pushed the thoughts away and tried to filter out the vibrancy of the turf from his vision. It was just grass and chalk lines. That's all it was.

He began to warm up with Alexei, doing wind sprints and stretching. Tyler glanced into the crowd, and the crimson overwhelmed him. The entire mass wore Krav colors. Arba had a substantial fanbase for the last game, but they hadn't come this time. Or maybe they had, and the Krav faithful had turned them away. Tyler wouldn't put it past them. The fans moved, a singular organism, breathing and singing as one. He scanned for Maria, but he couldn't see her. It would be finding a needle in a haystack.

The players warmed up. They all looked focused. Even the normally excited Grigore was doing less to psyche up the crowd, instead focusing on the players across the field, walking to his own teammates, talking to them quietly. Whatever happened today, both teams were ready.

Tyler felt Krav, right there, outside his fingertips. All he would have to do is try, and she would be there with him.

He held her away. He needed all of himself.

The match started. The crowd roared their approval, and Tyler focused only on the game that he loved.

Every player ran hard, pouring every ounce of themselves onto the field. Arba still had their quickness, dodging away from Krav who tried to dominate by getting in close and using their size to gain positional advantage. But Vlad wasn't lying when he said he would watch tape. Krav had adjusted. Instead of blindly running in with blunt pressure to take possession, they utilized multiple sequenced feints to force Arba's players to second guess themselves. And it worked. Krav consistently gained possession and put pressure on Arba's defense. They played a disciplined game and Tyler called no penalties on them.

Grigore darted through the Arba defense, took the ball, and scored, a thunderbolt off his foot. The crowd roared louder than Tyler had heard them. It was almost loud enough to hurt, the thousands in attendance all roaring at once at the top of their lungs. Krav had the lead.

It was short lived however. Arba began to adjust to Krav's strategy, and soon had multiple stretches of dominant possession, moving the ball up and down the field at will, the Krav players looking lost. The Krav goalie pulled some miraculous saves, keeping the sheet clean, but he could only do so much, for so long, with Krav's defense doing little. Arba scored, and the crowd screamed. It was a tie game in a game that could not end in a tie.

It stayed tied until halftime, after back-and-forth action, each team adjusting to the other. Both started playing sloppy, Tyler having to call multiple penalties on both teams and slowing the game down. The crowd yelled for blood every time he called a Krav penalty, but he ignored them. If they rushed the field, it'd be a forfeit for Krav. They would wait until the end to attack.

Tyler went into the locker room at halftime exhausted. The match was fast, and he was up and down the field. Alexei was a nice kid, and he had obeyed Tyler's orders, but he did not understand how to officiate. It was all up to Tyler. He drank some water and ate a light snack. He was burning up calories. He needed the energy.

The crowd never stopped. In fact, they only got louder, the stands shaking so much he worried they would collapse. The singing was heavier still, and it wasn't faint anymore, down in the locker room. It was clear as day.

YOU WILL LIVE FOREVER

Back out on the field, it overpowered him. He had to shout at Alexei to be heard, and the noise overwhelmed his whistle. When he blew to start the second half, he could barely hear it himself. The crowd tried to impose its will on the game. *Krav* tried to impose its will on the game.

Krav FC was doing its best to keep up, but just like the first game, their size came back to hurt them. The Krav players slowed down, their lungs not keeping their end of the bargain. Only Grigore maintained the same speed, tireless in his energy. Win or lose, he would not stop. Arba threatened multiple times, but they failed, Krav's defense doing enough to stymie them. Tyler called an offsides as Arba pushed to score, and the Arba coach got into a screaming match with him. Tyler screamed back, and after warning a yellow card, the coach backed down. Tyler called it down the middle.

Arba drove the ball down the field, and Krav began to collapse. Krav FC tried to execute the same feints as earlier in the game, but they weren't as crisp, and therefore no longer worked. Arba pushed past them, danced around Krav's defenders, and scored.

The crowd screamed again in anguish. Tyler felt the pain

this time. It was a deep ache, hurting inside him, somewhere so deep he couldn't reach. Only Krav could touch that place. She had been there while he marched with the faithful.

YOU WILL LIVE FOREVER

It was 2-1 and Arba threatened to pull away. But Grigore would not let them, willing Krav back into the game, dashing in with an extraordinary burst of speed and stealing the ball off a tightly clustered pack of Arba players. There were only a few players in front of him now, and each one bit on a hard cut, and then there was nothing but the Arba goalkeeper in between him and the back of the net. The goalie took a calculated risk then, coming out to try to take possession from Grigore. It was a risky move, but one that Grigore wouldn't expect.

And he didn't. The goalie was close, and Grigore saw what he was doing, understood now the play. The goalie went for a quick slice of the ball, just needing to make contact. Get it out of Grigore's orbit, and the scoring chance would be over.

Grigore saw him coming and did the first thing that came to mind. He kicked the ball as hard as he could. It was the right decision. He launched the football above the sliding goalie and it hit the back of the net, tying the game.

What happened next decided everything. The ball missed the goalie entirely, soaring right over his sliding body. Grigore's foot did not miss the goalie, however, kicking through the ball and directly into the Arba goalkeeper's face. It was much too late to stop it, and the goalie took the full force of Grigore's kick. His nose broke instantly, and he was out cold, unconscious on the field. The crowd roared first for the goal, and then again for the injury to the opposing team. The faithful didn't care that he was hurt, only that Arba would be without their starting keeper.

Tyler saw the whole thing, and for once, Grigore wasn't to blame. The goalie had put himself in that position and had paid the cost. The Arba players disagreed, and their lead striker was in Grigore's face immediately, screaming at him. Grigore didn't back down, and they were chest to chest, in each other's faces. Tyler had to stop them. The Arba player was courageous, but Grigore would kill him in a fight.

Tyler ran up, pushing through the fracas, trying to get everyone separated, finally finding himself at the center of it, at the back of the massive Grigore. Tyler shouted then, trying to break it up, but he couldn't be heard, no one could be heard, the crowd was louder than ever. Blood had been spilled, and the Krav faithful soaked it in, screaming emphatically, singing the Krav victory song, beyond singing, shouting the words aloud.

YOU WILL LIVE FOREVER

He finally put his arms around Grigore, trying to pull him away from the rest of the Arba players. If he could get Grigore out of the fray, it would die down, and they could finish the game. Grigore didn't appreciate the contact and swung his elbow as hard as he could backward, catching Tyler in the head, knocking him down. Grigore hadn't looked at who he was swinging at, he had just swung. Grigore glanced back, and saw that he had hit Tyler. His eyes went wide.

Tyler was dazed on the ground, but the rest was reflex. He reached for the red card, standing up, holding it high in the air. No touching the officials. Right down the middle.

If the crowd was loud before, it felt then as if the sound

had mass. Grigore was in his face now, the dispute with Arba forgotten. Arba tended to their wounded goalie while Grigore shouted in Romanian at Tyler. Tyler said nothing, only holding the red card aloft. Vlad came sprinting in then, not to shout at Tyler, but to separate the two. Grigore saw red, but Vlad grabbed him by the collar and forced him to break eye contact with Tyler.

Vlad pulled Grigore down to his level, speaking into his ear with purpose. Grigore's eyes softened, the anger disappearing. He nodded, took a deep breath, and walked off the field. Vlad followed him. The reaction surprised Tyler. What was Vlad's game?

It was simple after that.

Arba's goalie was replaced. So was Grigore.

Grigore was the best player on the field, and after he left, Arba dominated. Even without their starting goalie. Krav tried, every player doing everything they could, but they had no depth behind Grigore, and Arba scored two more goals. It was never close after that, and Tyler called the game after a few minutes of stoppage time. Krav never regained momentum.

The crowd knew they would lose before time ran out, but they let it finish. But they built up their own force, their own rage. They had been faithful, and they were rewarded for their faith with loss. It would not stand.

Vlad tried to stop them. It didn't work, and they poured onto the field. Tyler ran. Everyone did. It was mass chaos. Tyler saw the two thugs from earlier, and they were coming after him, but Tyler sprinted hard, even after a long and grueling match. Suddenly, he heard an engine, and he looked toward the noise to see a hatchback drive through the sets of chain-link fences that separated the field from the outside on the corners. It plowed through them, dodging groups of faithful, who did their own best to dodge the small car. It honked all the way. It headed for Tyler.

It skidded to a stop next to him. George's head poked out the window.

"Get in," he said. Tyler didn't wait for him to ask again, ripping open the door to the backseat and sliding in. George drove away before he shut it, leaving tire tracks in the field.

"I'm guessing they lost," said George.

"They did," said Tyler. "I called it right down the middle."

"The hard way," said George.

"Yes, the hard way," said Tyler. "Where's Maria? Is she okay?"

"She's back at my shop. We will collect her and then be on our way. She has your ID and phone. The road south is clear."

Relief washed through Tyler. A few people walked the streets, but George did not slow down on the short drive back. He honked the entire way, letting everyone know he was coming. He slid to a halt at his shop, knocking over some crates with the front bumper.

"Let's get her," said George. Tyler heard a sadness in his voice. He was leaving Krav for the first time in his life, and it was killing him. But he *was* leaving. They were all leaving.

Tyler hopped out with George, going inside. The lights were dim.

"Maria!" yelled Tyler. "Maria! Where are you?"

No answer, no sign of her.

"I thought you said she was waiting for us," said Tyler. He felt George behind him.

"I'm sorry, Tyler," said George. "But I would do anything for Krav."

Tyler felt a dull thud on the back of his head, and everything went black.

26

Tyler woke up inside the split circle. He struggled to breathe around the gag in his mouth. Figures in red robes surrounded him. His head ached. His wrists were bound together in front of him.

What had happened? He had been in George's shop. They had been escaping. And then--then George had betrayed him.

It was night. He could smell the smoke lingering in the air from the riots earlier. George stood in front of him, his hood removed.

Tyler stared at him, desperately. George only looked at him with sad eyes.

Tyler tried to talk through his gag, but it was impossible. No one paid attention anyway. Everyone looked to a new figure that walked up, putting a hand on George's shoulder. He revealed himself as Vlad, staring down on Tyler.

"You did what was best for Krav, old friend," said Vlad. "There is no shame in that. She will again be brought into the sun because of your effort." George stood up next to Vlad. Vlad put his arm around him. "It feels so good to have you back in the fold. We are so much stronger now. We are all connected once again. Let's get him on his feet." George and Vlad each grabbed him, pulling Tyler up.

Tyler tried to shake off the daze. The faithful surrounded him, hundreds deep in every direction. He couldn't see their faces. There was no way out. There was no way out. He glanced at Vlad. Vlad looked happy for the first time since Tyler had met him.

"It is a glorious day, Tyler!" said Vlad. "Can you feel it? It has taken so, so long for us to get Krav back to this point, but she is here, ready for what comes next. And we never would have gotten here without you, Tyler."

Tyler tried to speak again, but the gag muffled his words.

"I don't think we need that anymore, do we?" asked Vlad, and he untied the gag around the back of Tyler's head, pulling it away, handing it to a hooded figure behind him.

"Where's Maria?" asked Tyler. "What did you to with her?"

"Don't you worry," said Vlad. "She's doing well. It speaks to your character that she is the first thing on your mind. It's true with me as well."

"I didn't play your game, Vlad," said Tyler. "Krav lost. Another year in Level 4."

"Yes, that is true. We will not be promoted this year," he said. "To be honest, I didn't think we were ready at the beginning of the season. But with you Tyler, we will surely move up next season. With you, Krav will be great again."

"What?" asked Tyler. "Everything was riding on this game." He didn't understand, couldn't wrap his head around it.

"Well, yes and no," said Vlad. "Did you think I would put the success of Krav on a single match? We've worked much too hard to allow for that. And against Arba? They are an excellent team. And to come back from such tragedy. A terrific story. Everything was not riding on this game. Everything was riding on *you*."

"Yes, I know," said Tyler. "And I called it down the middle."

"Exactly!" said Vlad. "You proved me right. I am very proud."

"I--what?" asked Tyler.

"Grigore, come here," said Vlad, and a huge figure appeared, taking off his hood. It was Grigore. He walked up to Tyler and wrapped him in a giant hug.

"You did good, little chick," said Grigore, in his ear. "I am proud of you." He let go of Tyler, moving behind Vlad. He had the same smile as Vlad on his face.

"Grigore pushed you," said Vlad. "Sometimes maybe even a little too hard. But it worked out in the end."

"It was tough job," said Grigore. "But Vlad said it was necessary. For good of Krav. And he has always been right. And he was right again. And you are here, after everything. It is exciting! Our patience is being rewarded!"

"Calm down, Grigore," said Vlad. "We must show humility, for Krav. She will not want us to be boastful."

This didn't make sense. The game didn't matter? Grigore

pushing him? He was trying to align truth with reality, and he couldn't.

"I don't understand," said Tyler. He was looking around at the crowd of hooded figures, and they stayed still. Vlad stood with George and Grigore. "What's happening? Why the game? Why the blood?"

"Krav needs to feed," said Vlad. "But it cannot be on just anyone. That is the problem our ancestors made. They sacrificed too many, and it almost killed her. She was drowning. But there was a prophecy, made long ago, that when a hero and Krav came together in union, Krav would again be brought into the sun, and ascend into greatness. The hero and Krav would love each other, and through love and sacrifice, they would make Krav a god."

"I know. George told me about your prophecy," said Tyler, spitting every word. "But you can't fulfill it. You lost the game, you lost!"

"Oh Tyler," said Vlad. "The prophesied hero is not me. I am merely a servant to Krav. *You* are the hero."

"I don't understand," said Tyler. He felt manic, scatterbrained. His eyes darted from left to right, across the three faces to the shadowy figures. A hero? Love? "I'm no hero."

"You are that hero, Tyler," said Vlad. "You faced great challenges, physically, mentally, but you never backed down. You maintained your beliefs in the face of opposition. You saved a beaten stranger on the street. You redeemed a disheartened man. You stood up to a bully. You protected those weaker than you. If that is not a hero, what is?"

Memories flashed through Tyler's mind.

Don't be a hero.

Like action hero.

Are you volunteering, Mr. Hero?

You are what, American hero?

George approached him, meeting his wavery gaze. George embraced him, as tight as he had before. He spoke in his ear.

"I'm sorry, Tyler," said George. "I truly am. But what you said got through to me. And Vlad came to me. He apologized for leaving, so many years before. He said that he didn't want this great schism between us. And we talked. He told me about his sacrifice. I should have seen it. I--I have been so stubborn. So hard-headed. And he told me the truth about you and Maria. I understand now. I have all the pieces. Krav needs me, just like she needs you. Please forgive me. But I believe in Krav, and you understand. I know you do. You understand being a believer."

Tyler felt tears roll down his cheeks as George squeezed him a final time and moved back, next to Vlad and Grigore. Tyler still didn't understand.

"But--" he started. "But love? I do not love Krav. I was trying to flee. I wanted to leave this place behind forever."

"Do you deny our love, Tyler?" asked a voice coming from without the split circle, from the mass of hooded figures. Tyler recognized it.

No, please no.

The figures parted, letting one through, entering the split circle. She removed her hood and the rest of the crowd sunk to a knee. It was Maria.

"Maria," he said. "You--you betrayed me? I--I thought you loved me--" Tyler felt tears running down his cheek. She reached out and wiped them away.

"I do love you, Tyler," said Maria. "And I did not betray you. I am helping you fulfill your destiny. It is fate that brought you here. Fate that brought you and me together."

"You wanted to leave!" said Tyler. "We were going to escape Krav. Together. A clean break."

"I cannot leave Krav," said Maria. "I *am* Krav."

"What? No," said Tyler. "Impossible." His heart hurt. It took all his strength to stay on his feet.

"Why do think you felt such a connection to Krav, Tyler?" she asked. "Why you felt my blood beat beneath your feet? Because we were destined to be together. Our love connected us."

"But you are Vlad's daughter," he said. "You aren't Krav."

"She was once just my daughter," said Vlad. "Before we came here. But Krav had lost its avatar, under Stroescu. George's late wife could not bear the mantle. It killed her and Krav was without one for many years. I returned, and knew her avatar must be restored. A figure that would represent her in human form. So I gave her my daughter to inhabit. As recompense for all the time gone."

George's wife. With her long black hair, dying in her bed.

Krav had shown him. And he hadn't realized it.

Krav smiled. "And I forgave you and accepted your atonement. She has made a fine incarnation, one of the best I've ever had. Beautiful and strong."

"I never knew," said George. "I never knew. You sacrificed for us."

"I should have told you, old friend," said Vlad. "I let my pride come between us."

"I knew George would come around," said Krav. "It was only a matter of time."

Tyler's memory of the days before flashed in his mind.

Maria breaking down, her face contorting, strings of half sentences popping out of her. She had been trying to tell him. The real Maria. Somewhere deep inside this thing.

"She tried to warn me," said Tyler, his body aching. "She tried to tell me, but I didn't understand."

"She is a strong woman, still," said Krav. She smiled at Tyler. "But she is not Krav. She could not overpower me but for a few seconds, and only then, it was because I wasn't expecting it. After tonight, she will be locked inside forever. Tonight, after I become a god."

Tyler scanned their faces, all of them smiling, all of them happy. He screamed at them, starting to blubber.

"I loved you! What is wrong with you people? Nothing is worth this! Nothing is worth this!"

Krav looked at him with sympathy, again wiping away his tears.

"You would dare say that about these people's homes?" she asked, her beautiful face now alien to him. "Of course this is worth it. I will bring them into the sun. They will carry their town's name with pride. They will carry my name with pride. *Of course* it is worth it."

"I--I want to go home. Please, let me go home," he said, sobbing. Tyler tried to control himself. He searched for his center, but couldn't find it. The bottom had fallen out of him.

"Shh sh sh," said Maria, holding a finger to his lips. "You cannot leave, Tyler. You will stay here, forever. You and I will become one. You will ensure our future."

She smiled, and reached to Vlad. Vlad pulled the same dagger used to kill Dario, to kill Mark, from his robe, and placed it in Krav's open hand. Her fingers closed around it, lovingly. Vlad, George, and Grigore all knelt then, matching the hundreds of others who surrounded them.

She embraced Tyler. Tyler did nothing. All of his strength had left him.

"With you," she said, whispering into his ear. "I will break the world."

She stabbed him in the stomach, the dagger sinking into the hilt, and the last of Tyler's breath was driven out of him. With impossible strength, she pulled the blade up, sliding it vertically up Tyler's torso, cutting through skin, muscle and breastbone. With the dagger just under his throat, she pulled it out. He began to fall backwards then. She held him, with her other hand on the back of his neck, and lowered him gently to the ground. Tyler was still alive then, his breath gurgling out of him.

He looked up at the night sky. The stars were all he saw, the million pinpricks of light shining down on them. There was no moon tonight.

Krav knelt beside him, caressing his face with a bloody hand, before pulling him open, revealing his insides to that same sky. Tyler couldn't breathe anymore. He tasted blood. He felt her slip inside him. Her hand felt warm inside. Tyler could feel her close around him. She leaned down, her face now obscuring those stars. She was all he could see.

She kissed him then, deep and full of love, and ripped out his heart. Tyler died.

Krav held his heart aloft, blood trickling down her arm. With her other hand, she dug into the middle of the split circle. Her fingernails sank into the rocky earth, seeking something, going deeper and deeper. Inch after inch she dug until she found what she was looking for.

Blood began to well from the earth, like water. She could

feel its warmth. Here.

Krav lowered Tyler's heart into the hole, and she covered it, replacing the lost soil. She patted it down.

And then she felt it beat.

27

Two and a half years later.

Ryan Flynn had heard a lot about Krav before agreeing to the contract. He had heard about their tremendous rise into the second level of Drastovian football, the fanatical devotion of their fans, and a lot about the tiny town itself.

Mostly, that it was a shithole.

After they offered him the contract, he wanted to know what kind of town it was. What he got back was stories of potholes, and crumbling infrastructure, and a poor place that cared more about football than anything else. So that's what he was expecting when he came into town.

But it couldn't have been further from the truth. It was beautiful.

The roads were wide, recently paved, and pristine. New streetlights lined every street, with new street signs on every corner. A flag waved off of each one, adorned with a single symbol. A circle, with a line dividing it vertically. There was a massive new school on the east side of town, and a gorgeous park on the south, just north of the river that bordered the city limit. Children ran through the grass. It seemed every house had people out front, waving and smiling. Many of them flew the same flag, with the same circular symbol.

His driver dropped him at the stadium which towered over him. It seemed huge for such a small place. Vlad Popescu, the head coach of Krav FC, and apparently the mayor of Krav, waited for him there. Vlad's face was hard to read, but he seemed excited to meet Ryan.

"Welcome to Krav, young man," said Vlad, extending a hand. Ryan took it.

"Thank you," said Ryan.

"Ready to see where you'll play?" asked Vlad.

"Yes, of course," he said. "It's beautiful."

"Oh, thank you," said Vlad. "It's undergoing renovations."

"It looks quite new," said Ryan.

"It is," said Vlad. "But we're making it larger. Building it into a proper arena."

Vlad gestured and they started walking. Vlad unlocked and walked through an outer door, leading to an inner corridor. The walls were red.

"We're excited to have you Ryan," said Vlad. "We've never had a defender of your caliber. With you, we'll go straight to the top."

"Do you need me, though?" asked Ryan. "Anyone who's paying attention has seen your rise. Promoted twice in two years? Undefeated? It's unprecedented. Grigore's play alone--"

"The Bear is terrific, no doubt," said Vlad. "I consider him a son. But he can't carry the team forever. For us to get to the next level, we need more depth. We need more defense. And you can provide both of those things."

They continued walking, and then they were out on the field, and Ryan had to stop himself from shielding his eyes. The field was beautiful.

No, not beautiful. Transcendent. The color of the grass, the vibrancy of the green and white--it felt impossible. He had never seen anything like it.

"I--" he said. He struggled to find the words. "I've never--"

"We are very proud of our field," said Vlad. "It makes me smile every time I see it."

They walked out on it, and Ryan felt that same explosion underneath his feet, the vibrancy. The field felt alive, not just the grass as individual blades, but the field itself, as a creature unto itself.

"How does no one know about this?" he asked. "No one's mentioned this field."

"We like to think of it as the world's best kept secret," said Vlad.

They walked, and soon they were at midfield. The feeling of awe was even stronger here. Ryan looked down, and he saw it. The center circle. The same symbol that hung throughout town.

"They told me that the fans here were devoted, but for the town flag to have the center circle...that's a whole 'nother level," said Ryan.

"Oh, but it's the other way around," said Vlad. "That symbol has been a part of Krav for centuries. Long before football was even a sport."

"Really? Wow," said Ryan. "Then it almost seems like destiny that you'd end up good at football."

"You're right," said Vlad, with a gleam in his eye. "It does. I can sense your excitement. That makes me happy."

"I was a little apprehensive after all the stories I had heard about this town," said Ryan. "But everything looks great so far. Tremendous."

"Glad to hear it," said Vlad. "How about a drink?"

They were sitting down in a bar not ten minutes later, a short walk away.

"What's the name of this place?" asked Ryan.

"Bautura," said Vlad.

"Bautura," said Ryan. "I like it. Who's that, behind the counter? She's beautiful."

"That's Maria. My daughter," said Vlad.

"Shit. I'm sorry," said Ryan.

"Don't be," said Vlad. "She is the most precious thing in the world to me. She owns this place." Vlad put his hand to his mouth, miming telling a secret. "Don't tell anyone I told you this, but she secretly runs Krav. I just coach the football team." Vlad winked.

"Your secret's safe with me," said Ryan. Maria saw them and came over. Ryan had never seen a more beautiful woman, and her beauty increased with every step toward him. He had the same feeling as he had when he stood midfield, just minutes ago. A feeling of vibrancy. Of life. Of power. He caught himself holding his breath. She smiled at him.

"Who is this?" she asked, with an eyebrow raised. "Fresh

blood?"

"He is our new defender," said Vlad. "I am excited to have him."

"Oh, the troublemaker," said Maria. "Big news, your arrival."

"I see the rumor mill is already going to town," said Ryan. "I was hoping my past would stay that way, but I guess that was just wishful thinking."

"Just like you have heard things about Krav, we have heard things about you," said Vlad.

"I'm guessing they weren't all good," said Ryan.

"I had my suspicions," said Vlad. "But I try not to judge a man before I know him."

"I appreciate that," said Ryan. "For the record, whatever you heard is untrue. My last team--the locker room--it was a cesspool. I tried to do the right thing, tried to change the culture in there, and they wouldn't have it. Would rather cast blame on me and kick me out."

"Another thing I'm glad to hear," said Vlad. "I think you'll find Krav very welcoming. A couple of cold ones, darling, and a sandwich for Ryan here."

"Coming right up," she said.

"Any other foreigners here in Krav?" asked Ryan. "Your English is very good."

"Not at the moment," said Vlad. "But I think that will change with time. You'll find many of the townsfolk can at least understand English, if not speak it. It won't be a hindrance. I want Krav to grow, Ryan."

"It seems like it is," said Ryan. "Lots of new stuff. Schools, parks. It's great."

Vlad nodded. "You may be our first foreign player, but I

do not want you to be our last. I know you only committed for this season, but as it continues, I want you to consider staying for longer."

"I can't make any promises," said Ryan. "But I'll think about it." Before he stepped into town, Ryan had been considering this a year in purgatory. He'd do his time in Krav, perform well, and work his way back into civilization. But that field--and that bartender...

"Great!" said Vlad. "Regardless if you want to stay or not, you'll find that Krav welcomes all visitors as if they were one of our own. We have a long history, and a long memory for those who represent us."

Maria dropped off the beers, and Vlad raised his glass. Ryan met it.

"Even if you are done after your one year, you'll be a part of Krav forever."

Acknowledgements

Thank you to my wife Kim, for her patience and support, and my team of beta readers: Andrew, Matt, Megan, Yousef. Thank you for reading.

About the Author

Robbie Dorman believes in horror. The Split Circle is his fourth novel. When not writing, he's podcasting, playing video games, or petting cats. He lives in Texas with his wife, Kim.

You can follow Robbie on Twitter @robbiedorman

His website is robbiedorman.com

Subscribe to his newsletter at robbiedorman.com/newsletter

Enjoy The Split Circle?

Sign up here to be notified about Robbie's next novel!

robbiedorman.com/newsletter